MARY ELIZABETH

CUT BY THE COUNTY

Elibron Classics
www.elibron.com

Elibron Classics series.

ISBN 1-4021-7648-1 (paperback)
ISBN 1-4021-3403-7 (hardcover)

This Elibron Classics Replica Edition is an unabridged facsimile of the edition published in 1887 by Bernhard Tauchnitz, Leipzig.

COLLECTION

OF

BRITISH AUTHORS

TAUCHNITZ EDITION.

VOL. 2436.

CUT BY THE COUNTY BY M. E. BRADDON.

IN ONE VOLUME.

TAUCHNITZ EDITION.

By the same Author,

LADY AUDLEY'S SECRET	2 vols.
AURORA FLOYD	2 vols.
ELEANOR'S VICTORY	2 vols.
JOHN MARCHMONT'S LEGACY	2 vols.
HENRY DUNBAR	2 vols.
THE DOCTOR'S WIFE	2 vols.
ONLY A CLOD	2 vols.
SIR JASPER'S TENANT	2 vols.
THE LADY'S MILE	2 vols.
RUPERT GODWIN	2 vols.
DEAD-SEA FRUIT	2 vols.
RUN TO EARTH	2 vols.
FENTON'S QUEST	2 vols.
THE LOVELS OF ARDEN	2 vols.
STRANGERS AND PILGRIMS	2 vols.
LUCIUS DAVOREN	3 vols.
TAKEN AT THE FLOOD	3 vols.
LOST FOR LOVE	2 vols.
A STRANGE WORLD	2 vols.
HOSTAGES TO FORTUNE	2 vols.
DEAD MEN'S SHOES	2 vols.
JOSHUA HAGGARD'S DAUGHTER	2 vols.
WEAVERS AND WEFT	1 vol.
IN GREAT WATERS AND OTHER TALES	1 vol.
AN OPEN VERDICT	3 vols.
VIXEN	3 vols.
THE CLOVEN FOOT	3 vols.
THE STORY OF BARBARA	2 vols.
JUST AS I AM	2 vols.
ASPHODEL	3 vols.
MOUNT ROYAL	2 vols.
THE GOLDEN CALF	2 vols.
FLOWER AND WEED	1 vol.
PHANTOM FORTUNE	3 vols.
UNDER THE RED FLAG	1 vol.
ISHMAEL	3 vols.
WYLLARD'S WEIRD	3 vols.
ONE THING NEEDFUL	2 vols.

CUT BY THE COUNTY.

BY

M. E. BRADDON,

AUTHOR OF "LADY AUDLEY'S SECRET," ETC. ETC.

COPYRIGHT EDITION.

LEIPZIG

BERNHARD TAUCHNITZ

1887.

CONTENTS.

CUT BY THE COUNTY.

CHAPTER I.

"THE SHADE BY WHICH MY LIFE WAS CROST."

An English landscape. It seemed to Weldon Stukely that he had seen nothing so beautiful for the last seven years; and yet he had been where Nature has lavished her richest colouring, and her grandest forms. He had been a sojourner in the ancient world, the cradle of civilisation, of religion, language, science, art, poetry, and war—the immemorial East, from which antique Greece with all her glory was but an offshoot. He had been a traveller in the Himalayas, had looked upward at the unapproachable summit of Mount Everest: and now as the little hired landau from Scadleigh station came round a curve in a wooded road, and the village green, with its pond and herd of lazy kine, standing breast deep in the shining water, its old inn, and horse trough, and sign post, and three fine elms spreading their broad shadows on the patch of grass between the porch and the highway, and the labourers in their russet-brown frocks lounging on the stout oaken bench in front of the rough-cast wall—it seemed to the returning traveller as if this simple rustic landscape, this little picture of homely village life, surpassed all the loveliness of the tropics. And yet it was such a common-place scene—a scene we all know, which needs perhaps the glamour of a summer sunset, the feeling of eventide repose, to make it beautiful.

"Thank God for England," said Colonel Stukely, as he looked at the village green.

While he was looking back at it the fly drove in at the gates of Darnel Park, and a large matron was curtseying and smiling at him at the gate of her tiny lodge garden, a garden so crammed with flowers as to leave no room for the sole of a foot.

"How d'ye do, Mrs. Drabble?" said the Colonel, heartily as to an old friend. "As young as ever, but not any thinner, I see."

Mrs. Drabble laughed and shook her head. She had been a slim slip of a girl once upon a time, but it was so long ago that she had forgotten the sensation.

Darnel Park was one of those places which

leave within the mind an impression of perfect beauty, especially when seen for the first time in the summer sunset. It was full of fine old timber, and had those undulations and inequalities of surface which make a domain picturesque. The house was as old as Sir Christopher Wren, a delightful age for a country gentleman's mansion, as it allows of lofty ceilings, spacious rooms, plenteous light and air. Fine old oaks and beeches dotted the broad sweeps of grass, plantations of larch and Douglas fir sheltered the park from the outer world; while on one side of the house there was a wide expanse of broken ground, a region of deep hollows and craggy banks, mighty thickets of rhododendron and azalea, which Colonel Stukely called the jungle.

He was an expected guest at Darnel, but he had arrived by an earlier train than that by which he was supposed to travel; hence the hired fly, and hence also the fact that on alighting at the hall door he was told, apologetically, by Purdew, the old butler, that Sir Allan and Lady Darnel had not yet returned from their drive.

"There was a flower show at Walton, Colonel, and Sir George and my lady were obliged to be present. Your rooms are ready, Colonel. Shall I show you to them at once; or would you like to see Miss Darnel first? She is in the morning room expecting you."

"Miss Darnel," cried the Colonel eagerly. "Miss Grace, you mean?"

"No, sir; Miss Darnel—Sir Allan's sister, Colonel. I believe from a strict point of view," added the butler, gravely, deliberately, apologetically, "our own young lady is Miss Darnel, but Sir Allan's sister would never give in to it. I should never have the pluck to allude to *her* as Miss Dora."

Purdew was an old military servant of Sir Allan's. He had known the Colonel when Stukely and Darnel were brother officers, and felt himself privileged to chatter.

"Oh," said the Colonel, "Sir Allan's sister is in the morning room," as if the reminder of that lady's existence came upon him somewhat as a shock. "Yes, I will go and see Miss Darnel before I go to my room. My man will bring my portmanteaux on presently. I was in too great a hurry to wait for him."

He followed Purdew along a corridor, and into one of those gracious, home-like interiors which are the slow growth of generations; panelled walls mellowed by time, old Sheraton furniture, old Indian china, flowers in profusion; and on a scarlet Japanese table by the window an old-fashioned mahogany tea-tray, with brass handles, a George the Second tea-pot, and cups and saucers fresh from the royal factory at Worcester. Beside the tea table, with her face toward the door, smiling, expectant, sat a lady whose aspect was certainly not calculated to repel or alarm any man.

She was a little woman, fragile, gracefully fashioned, with a small face delicately tinted, light brown hair and dark brown eyes—fine eyes, penetrating, just a little imperious, the distinguishing feature in a face which might otherwise have been insignificant. She was daintily dressed in a pale grey gown of some soft gauzy material, the low tints of which harmonised exquisitely with her delicate complexion. Colonel Stukely knew that she was eight and thirty; but a stranger would as easily have believed that she was only eight and twenty. Happy result of having taken the utmost care of one's self under all the varied circumstances and agitations of life.

She welcomed the traveller with a gentle cordiality, a little touch of suppressed emotion, which ought to have been delightful to any man. But the Colonel was not enthusiastic. He had thanked God for the English landscape just now; but he had not the air of thanking God for Dora Darnel. He seated himself in the low reposeful chair she suggested to him; he took the offered cup of tea from her hand; but he was not demonstrative of delight in their meeting.

"I daresay you are rather surprised to find me here, *en permanence*," she said, "after Allan's marriage?"

The Colonel looked embarrassed for a moment or so; and then his natural gallantry came to his aid.

"I am surprised to find you still Miss Darnel. Our unworthy sex has been singularly blind to its own best interests."

"Your sex has not been neglectful of my claims, Colonel," answered the lady, laughing. "I have had opportunities of changing the name of Darnel—which I honour—for other names for which I do not care a straw. But I am not one of that silly herd of women who marry because they would rather be called Mrs. than Miss, who want a house of their own, forsooth; which is only another word for a burden of their own, a grinding care that shortens the lives of half the women in England. I am always angry when a girl, newly engaged to a man with nothing a year, talks to me of the delight of her having a house of her own. No, I am too contented with my fate as Dora Darnel ever to wish to change that name for another."

"I am so glad," the Colonel blurted out unawares, for he had been troubled seven years ago by a lurking suspicion that Miss Darnel meant to marry him. "I am so really glad you appreciate Allan's fine character, and that you are happy under his roof. It assures me upon one rather delicate point, namely, that you and the new wife get on nicely together."

Dora Darnel's face hardened for a moment, and then grew placid again. She had a sweet smile, a very sweet smile; but it was an idea of some physiognomists that the smile was too deliberately sweet to be quite genuine.

"Lady Darnel and I get on admirably," she said. "She found me the mistress of this house, possessing my brother's entire confidence as administrator of all household affairs, and finding that everything went as if by machinery, she was good enough——"

"Not to oust the engineer. She showed herself wise as well as amiable by taking that line," interrupted the Colonel, returning his cup for a second supply.

"She certainly acted with discretion," returned Dora, "for I do not think the poor thing had ever seen the inside of a well-appointed house before she came to Darnel."

"That's rather rough on her," said the Colonel.

"Do you mean to say that your brother has married a person who is—well—not quite a lady?"

"I do not go so far as that, Colonel Stukely: but my brother has married a woman of very charming manners, whose antecedents are a profound mystery to me and all our little world in Wiltshire."

The Colonel looked grave, distressed even. His old friend had been reticent about all the details of his new alliance—had only told his comrade that he had married one of the noblest of women, and that he was utterly happy in his marriage. That might mean anything or nothing. Every man thinks the woman of his choice the noblest of women; more especially if she is under a cloud when he marries her. Every man is utterly happy in his marriage for the first six months. So argued that old soldier, Weldon Stukely.

"Do you mean that Lady Darnel is not—received?" he gasped, after a pause.

"She is received, but she is not liked," answered Dora, leaning her pretty chin on her tapering hand, and looking the image of disinterested consideration. "People are cold. You know what county people are—how suspicious of anyone outside their own set, anyone not reared on their own soil, whose life they have not known from the cradle. People have been told absolutely nothing about Lady Darnel. We do not know who her own people are, or who her husband's people were. She appears to be an isolated person, without a relative or a friend — Clare, widow of Captain Stuart; no regiment, no locality, nothing to identify that one particular Stuart among the multitude that bear the same name. That was all the advertisement of her marriage told the county; that is all I, Allan's sister, have ever been told about his wife. Can you wonder that the county people do not take to her?"

"I can wonder at their stupidity if Lady Darnel is half as charming as I imagine her to be," protested the Colonel warmly.

"She is very charming. Perhaps if she were less attractive people would be less curious, less inclined to suspect evil. So handsome a woman ought to be able to reveal her antecedents, or else—"

"She is your brother's wife, Miss Darnel. You at least ought to respect her," said the Colonel, waxing angry.

"My dear Colonel, why fly into a passion?" exclaimed Dora innocently. "You have asked me questions, as an old friend of my brother's, and I have answered them frankly. Another time I shall know how to be diplomatic."

"There is one fact I gather from your answers, and that is that you are at one mind with the county in not liking Lady Darnel."

"Was there ever such a man for jumping at conclusions?" said Dora. "If this is the way you Indian officers treat your Sepoys no wonder they sometimes mutiny. Pray have I said that I don't like Lady Darnel?"

"Well, perhaps not in so many words. Suppose we change the subject, and you tell me about little Gracie, my god-daughter and plaything. I hope I am to see her this evening?"

"I expect to see her every minute. There is a tennis tournament at the Vicarage, and she is one of their best players—could not possibly be dispensed with—or she would have been at home to welcome her godfather. You will find her very much improved, I think."

"Not improved out of her old self, I hope. My dear little Robin Goodfellow in petticoats—the wildest, merriest lass, and the pluckiest little horsewoman in Wiltshire! Don't tell me that you have made a regulation young lady of her."

"We have done our best to make a lady of her, Colonel, however you may disapprove of the transformation. She ran wild at Darnel for a year after Allan's marriage. Lady Darnel was absurdly indulgent, quite the cleverest policy in a stepmother. She let the girl do just what she liked, and Grace would have become the scandal of the neighbourhood for her free and easy manners and want of cultivation if I had not interfered."

"Oh!" said the Colonel, "you interfered, did you?"

"It was my duty, as Grace's nearest female relative. At my suggestion my brother took her to Madame Sartori's finishing school at Passy. It is hardly to be called a school. Madame Sartori is a most accomplished person, who takes a few pupils—a chosen few. Only girls of good family are received; and they are trained under Madame's own eye. I was educated by her myself; and I can vouch for her care and vigilance."

"Poor Gracie! I can fancy her under Madame Sartori's vigilant eye. A wild wood-flower imprisoned in a Wardian case. I can imagine Madame Sartori—elderly, snuffy, suspicious. Poor Gracie! And how long was she subjected to the Sartorian process?"

"She spent two years in Paris, with occasional holidays at home. The result is eminently satisfactory to Sir Allan."

"And are Grace and her stepmother still good friends?"

"They are—or pretend to be—intensely fond of each other."

"I cannot imagine Grace pretending anything, unless Madame Sartori's process has made her a new creature."

"Madame Sartori has transformed a hoyden into a young lady."

"Oh, what a pity!" sighed the Colonel. "England swarms with young ladies; but your true hoyden is a rare growth, a plant that can only flourish in the genial soil of a happy home, a gracious flower that withers under the breath of the schoolmistress. I am heartily sorry you ever sent my Gracie to school. I hate girls' schools."

"Madame Sartori's could hardly be called a school," repeated Miss Darnel. "I was under her care myself, and I ought to know the value of her training."

Colonel Stukely looked at the speaker curiously. Yes, she was undoubtedly the outcome of the carefullest training — moved, spoke, smiled by rule. Could enter or leave a room gracefully. Had no awkward tricks of speech or deportment. Played a little, sang a little, danced elegantly, spoke French and Italian with perfect intonation, a precisian in all things.

"Trained too fine," thought the Colonel.

Just then a light, swift figure flitted across the lawn, and bounded in at the window, a figure all in white, soft white woollen stuff, bordered with pale blue, the most charming thing in tennis frocks. This was Grace Darnel, a tall slip of a girl, with sunny hazel eyes, and rippling auburn hair, lovely mouth, and perfect teeth; other features inoffensive; a true English type.

"Gracie," said the Colonel, after he had taken both her hands and shaken them heartily for a minute or so, contemplating the fair young face with fatherly affection, "Gracie, they tell me you have grown into a young lady, and that my little Robin Goodfellow is gone."

"Then they have not told you the truth, godfather. I shall always be Robin Goodfellow for you," answered the girl, smiling at him.

And then after a little pause she said—

"I am so glad you are come home, more glad than I can tell you."

She said this with an earnestness which half suggested some hidden meaning. The Colonel looked at her scrutinisingly with his keen, kind eyes—eyes that had looked just as steadily in the face of mutiny and murder in the days that were gone.

Miss Darnel had glided from the room, and they two were alone together.

"Why, Grace, that sounds as if you were not quite happy," he said anxiously.

"Who is quite happy in this world?" retorted Grace, with a touch of petulance. "It is an impossible condition. We are told in church every Sunday that we are not intended to be happy—though why we should be born for the express purpose of being miserable is more than I am able to understand. But I am very happy at having you back again, godfather. There is no alloy to that gold."

"My dearest child, do you not suppose that I am just as glad to return? And now tell me everything. Remember what changes have taken place since I last saw Darnel, and that I come back to you a stranger in knowledge of your domestic affairs, though no stranger in feeling. Tell me about the stepmother."

"Hush, godfather, we never use the qualification 'step' before the word mother. I call Lady Darnel my mother, and by no other name. She is the first woman who ever gave me a mother's love. You know that my own dear mother died when I was a baby, and that I have only her picture to love. There is no disloyalty to her in being fond of my new mother."

"Then Lady Darnel is nice, that is a grand point."

"Lady Darnel is simply perfect as wife and mother; and before you have been in this house twenty-four hours you will be over head and ears in love with her. Father won't be angry. He is too proud of seeing her admired."

"I am charmed to hear such an account; and yet Miss Darnel spoke of her just now with a certain reservation?"

"When did you ever hear Aunt Dora speak of anyone or anything without a certain reservation?"

"But, Gracie, with such a mother, and such a father, you ought to be supremely happy."

Grace blushed, and looked up at him shyly.

"Don't you know, Colonel, that there comes a time in every girl's life when even father and mother are not quite all the world to her."

"I understand," said Weldon Stukely. "There is a lover in the case."

The very sound of the word, blurted out pointblank in the soldier's hearty voice, seemed to appal Grace Darnel. She glanced at the window.

"Not one word, not one breath," she whispered, clasping her hands entreatingly. "It is a secret. Nobody knows. My father would never forgive—Hark! there is the carriage, and I must rush off to dress for dinner."

She was gone before he could say another

word. He went out after her, and met Sir Allan and his wife in the hall.

Sir Allan had retired from the army ten years ago, upon the death of his father, from whom he inherited Darnel Manor and half-a-dozen of the best farms in the Vale of the White Horse. He had retired invalided, and he was slightly lame even now from the effects of a bullet in Cabul. Weldon Stukely and he had been together at Eton, as brother officers had fought side by side in the Crimea, and had borne the heat and burden of the Indian Mutiny. They had been comrades and friends in the golden days of youth, and they loved each other like brothers. Their meeting was full of quiet tenderness, undemonstrative, as became two Englishmen.

"Weldon, my wife," said Sir Allan, and the Colonel turned to greet Lady Darnel.

She was a beautiful woman, in the prime of womanhood, just eleven years Sir Allan's junior. The tall, graceful figure, the finely-cut features, low broad brow, and dark grey eyes, had a look of quiet dignity which well became the mistress of Darnel Manor. Not a woman this for the county to cut, thought Weldon Stukely. Not a woman to awaken suspicion in the minds of the most punctilious of village rectors or the most prejudiced of squires. She looked like a woman born to command homage, to inspire affection, an ideal wife and mother.

She was simply dressed; more plainly than women of her station are wont to dress upon public occasions; but the finely moulded figure, the beautiful face, gave importance to the black foulard gown and neat little chip bonnet. People at Darnel had an idea that everything Lady Darnel wore came direct from Paris, and that this simple attire of hers was more costly than other people's finery.

"Catch a woman of that stamp saving her husband's money," they said to each other, over their afternoon teacups.

Nobody had ever explained what particular stamp or character of person was meant by this vague phrase; but it was an understood thing that Sir Allan Darnel had married a nobody, and that it was in the nature of things he should come to rue his marriage. The county had not been taken into Sir Allan's confidence when he married; the favours of the county had not been solicited for the new firm; and the county was therefore of one opinion, expressed freely among the feminine portion of the community.

"There is evidently something," said the county.

"It will all come out before long," said the county.

Everyone was sorry—laboriously sorry—for Sir Allan; all the more so because Sir Allan persisted in not being sorry for himself. He went up and down the village beaming with content. His voice was the cheeriest in the hunting field. He was in excellent spirits at Quarter Sessions, and inclined to let offenders off lightly, from very lightness of heart.

"Why should we be hard upon these poor devils?" he would plead. "Their lives are so miserable, and ours are so happy."

"There will be some painful scenes at the Manor before we are many years older," said the county. "Poor Sir Allan is an absolute fool; and a wife of that kind will naturally take advantage of such a husband's weak indulgence."

"I am told that Mason charges five-and-thirty pounds for a foulard gown like that she wore on Tuesday," said the Dowager Lady Brumpus.

The foulard gown was made by a little dressmaker in Pimlico, who had worked for Lady Darnel when she was Mrs. Stuart; but the county had its own sources of information, which were almost always false.

"Welcome to the Manor," said Sir Allan's wife, with her hand in the Colonel's. "I hope you are going to stay with us for a long time."

"I hope he is going to stay with us till he

finds a snug little place of his own within a couple of miles, and that he will settle down there for the rest of his life," said Sir Allan.

In one of his latest letters the Colonel had talked of wanting to buy a place near his friend's. His period of service was over, had been extended to the uttermost limit by especial privilege; but that limit was past, and the stalwart soldier, in the prime of manhood, had to lay aside his sword, or turn it into a ploughshare.

"Yes, Allan, I mean to settle near you, if I can, and to look after my goddaughter. That is about the only business I can find in life henceforward."

"Unless you follow my example," said Sir Allan cheerily.

Lady Darnel had left them. Sir Allan conducted his old chum to the rooms that had been prepared for him—bedroom, dressing-room, and study—three of the prettiest rooms in the spacious old house; a study with a bow window overlooking the pastoral side of the park, where Lady Darnel's particular herd of Jersey cows browsed peacefully in the low western light, fetlock deep in the rich grasses of late summer. The bow window had been broken out thirty years before, and was considered a blot, from an architectural point of view; but it made that cosy little study the nicest room in the house.

It was seven o'clock when Sir Allan left his guest, and the Colonel had an hour in which to dress for dinner in a leisurely way that gave him full scope for meditation. Naturally it was of his friend and his friend's wife that he thought.

"She is very handsome," he told himself, "and she is a good woman. I would stake my life that she is true as steel. But she is not happy. There is the rub. There is a mystery. I don't wonder the county people talk. A woman in Lady Darnel's position—with such a husband as Allan—and such Jersey cows"—his glance wandered involuntarily to the fawn-coloured, black-muzzled herd in the pastures yonder—"a woman in Lady Darnel's position ought to be happy: and if she is *not*—well, if she is *not*, there is a reason."

He recalled that calm, finely-cut face, its proud repose, its look of serious thought. No, and again no, it was not the countenance of a happy woman. Allan might rejoice in his destiny, might deem himself blessed among men: but there was a secret canker gnawing the heart of Allan's wife.

"Stuart?" muttered the Colonel presently, "Widow of Captain Stuart? What Stuart, I wonder?"

And then he began to recall the men of that

name whom he had known in the service. They were numerous; but he could remember none of them likely to have left a beautiful widow. And why had not her husband's regiment been mentioned in the advertisement?

"There must be some screw loose," said the Colonel.

He found the three ladies and his old chum in the drawing-room when he went down: no one else.

"I would not have anybody asked for to-night, Weldon," said Sir Allan; "for I knew that you and I would want to talk: and it's hard lines for other men to sit by while a couple of Anglo-Indian fogeys go over their old stories together."

Dinner was announced almost immediately. The Colonel took Lady Darnel to the dining-room, and sat between her and Grace, while Miss Darnel occupied the other side of the snug oval table in solitude. Sir Allan and his daughter were in high spirits, full of old reminiscences, hunting and horses, Grace's ponies and Grace's dogs, which seemed to be legion; the old men and women who had died since the Colonel went back to India; the changes in the village, the new school-house.

"Talking of schools, how is it you have not told me anything about Paris and your experiences there?" said the Colonel. "It must have been a tremendous change from Darnel Park to the Bois de Boulogne."

Grace blushed furiously, and was silent for a moment or two.

"Did you like Passy and your French schoolmistress?" asked the Colonel.

"I detested being sent there," replied Grace, flashing an angry glance at her aunt, whom she had never forgiven for that act of interference, which had in somewise changed the girl's destiny, "and I saw no reason why I should be sent to school—at my age. But I got to like the place pretty well afterwards. Madame Sartori is a silly old woman; but she did not ill-treat us, or interfere with us much. Her house was Liberty Hall, And I was sent there to be drilled and trained as if it had been a reformatory. That was a capital joke."

She laughed a bitter little laugh, and her voice had a hard tone which Colonel Stukely did not like. Was this his sweet ingenuous Gracie; the girl who was the soul of simplicity and truth? He felt that there was a change—an evil change—wrought by that accursed Parisian school. He had always hated Paris; he had always hated girls' schools. If heaven had given him daughters he would have let them grow up in the meadows, like those Jersey cows—in the hunting field—on the river. He would have had them taught reading and writing, perhaps, in the winter evenings. No more. He would at any rate have reared a healthy brood.

"In *my* time Madame Sartori was quite the most perfect person in her ways with girls," said Dora Darnel.

"Ah, but your time was so very long ago, Aunt Dora," answered Grace. "There has been time for Maman Sartori to outlive all her gifts since then."

"Nor in my time did anyone ever think of calling her Maman Sartori."

"Ah, girls were so dull and prim twenty years ago," retorted Grace. "Youth has only learnt to live since the last decade. American girls have taught us our rights, and how to enjoy them."

"Gracie!" exclaimed her father, with a reproachful look. "You are not talking like my daughter."

"I beg your pardon, father," the girl answered hastily, "but I always feel mad when people talk to me about that horrid villa at Passy—with its shallow gentility—and its shams of all kinds."

"Then I am the offender," said the Colonel, "for it was I who started the subject. I shall be wiser in future."

"You were not prepared for the effects of American emancipation," remarked Dora, in her soft girlish voice, a voice that had never been heard raised in anger within the memory of anybody at Darnel Manor; and yet that dove-like murmur was associated with some of the bitterest speeches that had ever been spoken at Darnel.

Lady Darnel came to the rescue, and turned the conversation into a new channel by questioning the Colonel about his last campaign; whereupon the talk became animated again, and went on pleasantly until the ladies withdrew, and the two old friends were sitting opposite each other alone in the lamplight.

"Light your cheroot, Weldon. I suppose you stick to Colonel Newcome's old weed—or will you have one of my cigarettes?" inquired Sir Allan, offering his exquisitely embroidered case, the sort of thing with which a man like Allan Darnel is provided to satiety by his womankind.

"And now, dear old fellow, tell me frankly how do you like her?"

"Thank God, I can afford to be frank. To see Lady Darnel, for the first time even, is to like and admire her. She is beautiful, she is charming, she is all I should wish my old friend's wife to be, only——"

"Only what, Weldon? You have discovered a drawback already."

"Not to Lady Darnel's merits. But it struck me that her health and spirits are not quite so good as you and her friends would wish."

"You are right. No, my poor Clare is not in robust health. There is something—a depression—a nervous excitability sometimes. I doubt if Darnel Manor agrees with her. We have lived here too exclusively, perhaps, since our marriage, I have been thinking seriously of taking her to Italy for the winter. No, her spirits are too variable for good health, or for ease of mind. But there are reasons—cruel memories of the past which in a measure account for this. I have not yet told you the story of my marriage, Weldon."

"You told me very little; only that your marriage was a love match, and that you were supremely happy. That was enough to satisfy your friend."

"But I should have told you a good deal more if it had not been for my aversion to letter writing. It was a longish story to write, and a painful one; so I thought it would be easier to tell you all about it when you and I were smoking our cigars face to face, as we are to-night."

"Don't tell me one word, if there is a shade of sorrow in the recital," said the Colonel earn estly. "I am content to know that Lady Darnel is a good and beautiful woman. I desire to know nothing beyond that."

"My dear fellow, it will be a relief to talk to you. I want you to appreciate Clare, and to understand her: and you can only do that when you know her sad story."

The Colonel bowed, and filled his glass with Léoville.

"Do you remember hearing eleven or twelve years ago of an officer of the 19th Afghanistans, a man called Mackenzie?"

"The man who shot the sentry? Certainly I remember hearing of him. Everybody heard of him—a terrible case."

"The man who shot the sentry was my wife's first husband."

"Good Heavens!"

"Yes; he was her first cousin. Stuart Mackenzie, a man who began life brilliantly, who was a celebrity in his way for two or three seasons, as one of the handsomest young men in London. Perhaps that spoiled him. His father died before he was of age, and he succeeded to a handsome fortune, which he began to squander directly it came into his possession. Clare's mother was a widow, a woman of the world, had been a beauty, lived only for society, and cared very little for her daughter. I have gathered as much as this from Clare's reluctant admissions, rather than from actual statement, as she has been loth to cast the faintest reproach upon her dead mother."

"I know the kind of woman," said Stukely, "not by any means an uncommon type."

"Clara was only seventeen, and had not yet been introduced into society, wore school-girl frocks, practised Beethoven, and read Schiller with a good old governess, while her mother went to parties. They spent the London season in a West End lodging, and lived for the rest of the year at Torquay, where Mrs. Molyneux, Clare's mother, had a house of her own. The widow's means were limited, and just sufficed for this kind of life; and I daresay she looked forward with a dread to the expense of launching a pretty daughter, still more perhaps to the idea of being outshone and aged by the daughter's appearance. Anyhow, she kept Clare very close; and when Stuart Mackenzie proposed for his cousin, Mrs. Molyneux received him with open arms, and forced on the marriage with all the strength of a mother's influence. Clare, who was at first reluctant, was gradually persuaded to think herself very fond of her cousin. He and she had been playfellows in her childhood, and she had liked him very well then. It was flattering to think that one of the handsomest young men in London was over head and ears in love with her. The idea of immediate escape from the governess, the German poets, and the dulness of London lodgings was pleasanter still. The prospect of a voyage to India was sheer enchantment. The girl gave way. The marriage was hurried on, as the Afghanistans were under sailing orders within six weeks. Clare spent her honeymoon in Italy, and sailed with her husband from Trieste in a great troop-ship a fortnight after her wedding-day, and six months before her eighteenth birth-day."

"Poor child."

"The life in India was gay and bright enough at the first. There had been rumours of war, but nothing came of those rumours. India was supremely quiet in that long lull which followed the suppression of the Mutiny. Gradually, slowly, the sickening truth dawned upon my poor Clare. She had married a profligate, a spendthrift, and a gamester. She shrinks with horror from all memories of that hateful life; yet there have been times when it has seemed a relief to her to talk to me about those days, when the over-burdened mind has thrown off some part of its load; and at such times I have encouraged her confidences. Her husband was one of the most popular men in India from a social standpoint, during those first few years. He was brilliant, fascinating, clever, open-handed; but he was a thoroughly bad man all the same, and his wife was the chief sufferer by his vices. Then came a change. Intemperate habits told their usual tale. He grew nervous, excitable, short-tempered, most of all when he had been unlucky at play; and play was his nightly amusement. He became very unpopular with his brother officers; and the feeling of the mess at last came to a point which rendered an exchange inevitable. Mackenzie exchanged from the famous Afghanistans into a line regiment quartered in the south of Ireland."

"A dreary change, I should think," said Stukely, whose happiest years had been spent under an Indian sun, to whom the ways of Indian life were the familiar ways, and those of Britain strange.

"A change that wrecked him for ever. In India there were some restraining influences—caste, society, the knowledge that the eyes of great men were upon him; but in that shabby little Irish town there were none. He sank into a dull apathy—abandoned every ambition of an honourable man—sulked with his wife—was foolishly indulgent one day, brutally harsh the next, to their only child, a boy of seven, and the wife's solitary consolation. He had spent nearly all his money. He had thrown away all his chances of advancement. He knew this; and the very knowledge that he was a ruined man made him reckless. He drank to drown care—drank till his brain grew soddened and dull—drank until delirium tremens became a chronic malady. Oh, the horror of those days, as Clare describes them. The ever recurring evil, which she dreaded in every hour of her life. She was his nurse when he was ill. She screened him—she apologised for him—she enabled him to keep his position years after his own folly would have forfeited it. They went from station to station—now at home, now abroad—and it was on their return to that dull old town in the south of Ireland that the catastrophe occurred which gave Stuart Mackenzie's name a criminal notoriety."

"I remember. It was at Mallow the murder occurred."

"The crime was hardly to be called a murder, for the wretch was mad when it happened. He had been laid up for a week with an attack of delirium tremens which was a little worse than any previous experience in the same line. His orderly was a good fellow, young, stalwart, plucky, and Clare and the orderly contrived between them to nurse him and to keep everything dark, though his paroxysms were at times so violent as to need all the orderly's strength and all Clare's courage to grapple with him. Things went on like this for a week, by which time both servant and mistress were fairly worn out, while there were no signs of improvement in the patient. The doctor knew what the complaint was, but did not know half the violence of the attack, so careful was Clare to conceal the worst symptoms—a mistake, as she discovered afterwards."

"I can understand that look in Lady Darnel's face now," said the Colonel, meditatively; "the look of a woman who has suffered intensely in years gone by, and who can never quite forget the old wounds."

"Perhaps neither Clare nor the servant knew how utterly exhausted they both were by what they had done and gone through in that dreadful week, for when Clare left the man on guard one night, and went to her room for a few hours' rest, she had perfect confidence in his watchfulness. The poor fellow dropped asleep at his post. It was a moonlight night in summer, and Mackenzie's window opened on to a balcony. The trooper had locked the door, and put the key in his pocket. But to a man of Mackenzie's athletic training the descent from that first floor balcony was easy. He saw his keeper asleep, saw himself unwatched for the first time since his malady had come upon him, and, delighted at the idea of freedom, he got up, dressed himself hastily in trousers and shooting jacket, scaled the balcony, and made for the gates of the barracks. At the gate he was challenged by a sentinel, who did not recognise him. Mackenzie did not answer the challenge, and the soldier tried to stop him. He wrenched the gun out of the sentinel's hands, and shot him through the head. The sound of the shot in the silence of the night awakened the men in the quarters nearest the gate. There was an alarm, and the sentry was found dead in front of his box. Mackenzie was not found till late on the following afternoon, when he was discovered hiding in a wood five or six miles from the barracks, with the sentry's gun in his hand—stark mad. There was a trial, which resulted in Captain Mackenzie's detention during Her Majesty's pleasure; but he only lived a little more than a year after his transference to the county asylum, where Clare visited him every week. He never recovered from that shock, and the exposure of that night. He sank into a state of melancholy madness, in which his nights were haunted by horrible dreams—always acting over again that struggle for the gun with the sentry—

always shooting him and seeing him fall, shot through the brain—not one sentry but a hundred sentries—till he woke in agony, steeped in cold sweat which he mistook for blood. He used to tell Clare these dreams—with an awfully graphic power which tortured her. He became singularly mild in those days—drivelling and imbecile in his lunacy, save when he was excited by the thought of those nightly visions. Clare asked his keeper if he had these dreadful dreams every night, and the man told her he had never known a night go by without his being awakened by that cry of horror—'the sentry!' Death came at last, by inches, a gradual extinction of mind and body. Dissolution in its most painful form."

"What a martyrdom for a wife!"

"Yes, a veritable martyrdom; but her sorrows were not over. She was left poorly off, with one child, her boy, her comfort and consolation in the earlier years of his life, but already, at eight years old, a trouble and an anxiety. The child was rebellious, difficult, fitful, alarmingly like his father in person and disposition. Clare's mother was dead, and she stood alone in the world. She dropped the name of Mackenzie, and called herself Stuart. She went to a quiet little inland watering-place in Mid-Wales, and devoting herself to her boy, gave up her whole life to the task of training him until it should be time for him to go to a public school. Her own education had been carried further than the average standard by her conscientious German governess, and she was able to prepare her boy for Rugby. She made up her mind that he should not be a soldier. She wanted to shield him from the temptations of army life. He went to Rugby, she pinching herself to provide the expenses of his maintenance there; and he was expelled in the second year. That was a crushing blow. Then he told her that he had not tried to do well. He had set his heart upon being a soldier, and she had better send him to an army coach to prepare for Woolwich. That profession, and no other, would he work for. She was firm, and the boy was sullen. If he was not to go into the army he would do nothing. He idled away his life in the little Welsh settlement, amusing himself with any sport that came within his reach—fishing, shooting, a day's hunting now and again—always a trouble and an expense, a care and a grief to the poor mother. But the worst was to come. Before his nineteenth birthday she had discovered the hereditary taint. Her son was an incipient drunkard. She moved heaven and earth to get him into new surroundings, a more active life. She was told by a medical wiseacre that a new country, an open air life would cure him; and after infinite trouble she shipped him off to Queensland, with introductions which provided for his being decently placed at a sheep-farmer's when he got there. She heard from him once after his arrival, a letter written in good spirits, full of sanguine ideas of success in his new career. And then followed a silence which has never been broken; but in the account of the Erl King, bound from Brisbane to London, there was in the list of passengers lost a young man called Stuart, travelling alone, whose description, obtained by Clare from the Brisbane agent, corresponded very fairly with that of her son, so it is more than probable that the sea has closed over Valentine Stuart."

"Let us hope it is so," said the Colonel cheerily; "a young man with those proclivities could never be anything but a scourge to the mother. For your sake, and for Lady Darnel's, I hope the youth found a watery grave. There is something very terrible in the idea of death when it takes away someone we love; but there is something uncommonly comfortable in the idea of death when it removes someone we want to get rid of," added the Colonel philosophically. "Death is so thorough!"

"It was at Torquay that I met my wife," continued Sir Allan. "I went there after a month with the Exmoor Hounds, for a few days' visit to an old friend of my father's, vicar of one of the outlying parishes, a man who remembered Hurrell Froud and the days of the Oxford Tracts. He had known Clare from her childhood, had prepared her for confirmation, and married her to the man who blighted her life. I heard the sad story from him before I saw her face. Perhaps sympathy and compassion prepared my heart for loving her. In any case, I fell in love with her at first sight, and I did not leave Torquay till I had won her. I am bold enough to believe that her heart was mine almost from the beginning; but she was constrained by unselfish fears for my welfare, and it was with difficulty I obtained her consent to be my wife with as little delay as possible. She feared the scandal that might arise in my neighbourhood if once that terrible story of her first husband got wind; she reminded me of the uncertainty surrounding her son's fate, and the possibility he was still living, and might be a burden and a disgrace to me in the future. I told her that these things were trifles—feathers when weighed in the scale against the gold of true love. In a word, I overruled all her objections, laughed her fears to scorn; and six weeks after our first meeting the dear old vicar married us, and we started in the dull gray November weather for our honeymoon tour across the Cornish moors, and along the wild sea-coast from Tintagel to the Lizard. Oh, those happy days in the little inn at the Land's End, beside the roaring Atlantic! alone, remote from the world and its ways. I shall never forget the sweetness, the perfect confidence and love of that time. It has grown and strengthened since then—it will go on increasing till I die."

"And there has been no cloud on your happiness at Darnel?"

"None, or only the lightest summer clouds hardly worth talking about. My marriage was naturally a blow to Dora, who had been mistress of Darnel Manor ever since my stepmother's death. She talked at first of going away—living abroad—taking a house in Salisbury, for the sake of the Cathedral service, she said. But she stayed on, interfered a good deal with my wife in the management of the house and servants, and was obviously unhappy."

"You ought to have got rid of her, Allan," said the Colonel, frankly. These *ménages à trois* never answer. It would have been happier for you and your half-sister if she had set up an independent establishment, were it even within a mile of your gates."

"I was seriously meditating making her the

offer of a handsome addition to her income, in order to enable her to live independently, without any diminution of the comfort she has enjoyed here."

"So like you, my dear Allan, to be seriously meditating a step which ought to have been taken months before you began to meditate," said the Colonel, laughing.

"Well, I do not want to be unbrotherly, you see; and Dora had kept my house so admirably. However, while I was thinking of cutting the knot of the difficulty my way, my dear Clare cut it her way, which was much more generous. She came down to breakfast one morning with her little morocco key-casket in her hand, and gave it over to Dora in my presence. 'I am a very bad housekeeper,' she said, 'and I have no love for government, while you are a superb manager and have rather a liking for the reins of power; so why should we live uncomfortably when we might live happily, each after her own taste? From this day forth I renounce all administrative rights and privileges at Darnel Manor.'"

"How did Miss Darnel take that?"

"Hardly so pleasantly as she ought to have done. She sneered at poor Clara's renunciation of domestic management, as if it had been an assertion of intellectual superiority. 'I daresay looking after servants and ordering dinners does seem a very degrading occupation to a person of your superior mind,' she said, 'but I have always remembered that my brother's comfort depends upon these vulgar details.' She made me very angry."

"I should have taken her by the scruff of the neck and pitched her out of doors," interjected Colonel Stukely.

"I did not go quite so far as that, but I gave Dora a bit of my mind there and then; and I think her cold ham and chicken that morning was rather a hot breakfast. She is always sweetest after a good licking; so after breakfast she took the keys as meekly as a lamb, and promised that she would prove worthy of Lady Darnel's confidence. 'You are much too generous and too indulgent to the servants,' she said. 'That has been your only fault as a housekeeper.'"

"A change had come o'er the spirit of her dream," laughed the Colonel. "Ten o'clock, by Jove. Hadn't we better go to the ladies?"

CHAPTER II.

"WE PLAY WITH LIGHT LOVES IN THE PORTAL."

COLONEL STUKELY had been a guest at Darnel Manor for nearly two months. He had explored all the country side, within thirty miles, looking for that ideal estate—a small but perfect house, with perfect stables, a good old-fashioned garden, and about forty acres of fertile pasture—which he had dreamed of for many a year under the tropic stars, and which he found almost as difficult of attainment as if he had wanted an estate in one of those very stars. The Colonel and his host drove many a mile in Sir Allan's dog-cart with the high-stepping horse, to see places which were described in auctioneers' advertisements as earthly paradises, and which generally proved the kind of habitation that a man buys in an interval of lunacy, with insane ideas of improvement or reconstruction, and which he tries to shuffle off upon a new victim directly he recovers his senses.

The Colonel made shorter pilgrimages in his god-daughter's pony carriage, Gracie very proud of driving her warrior about the country. But as yet nothing beyond the pleasure of exploring a charming landscape in the golden harvest time had resulted from their excursions.

Yes, there had been one result, and an important one, so far as Grace Darnel was concerned. During one of these rustic jaunts the girl took courage and opened her heart to her godfather, the most faithful and the most indulgent friend she had ever known from the days of her childhood.

They went a little further than usual on this occasion, to a place which had been described as a gem of picturesque beauty; and which turned out to be a dilapidated farmhouse situated on the edge of a swamp, and surrounded by meadowland that would have cost a small fortune to drain. The Colonel was amused rather than indignant at the discrepancy between the place itself and the auctioneer's advertisement, and laughed heartily at his own disappointment.

"To think that we should have driven eleven miles through some of the vilest roads in Wilts to look at such a god-forsaken hole as this," he exclaimed, after he and Grace had perambulated the neglected old garden and had emerged upon the road in front of the gates.

There was a long wooden bridge a few paces further on, spanning an expanse of watery pasture, full of reed and bulrush, and on this bridge the Colonel stood, with his arms folded on the hand-rail, looking lazily at the lazy kine standing up to their haunches in the rank verdure.

He turned round, smiling at his goddaughter, expecting her to be amused at this latest example of house agents' inventive faculties; but to his surprise and discomfiture he found her in tears.

"Why, Gracie," he cried tenderly, "what is amiss with my little girl?"

"Everything," Grace answered vehemently. "I must tell some one. I cannot bear it any longer. To be so base, so secret, so false to those I love! I hate and despise myself. I really think I am the wickedest, meanest girl in England. I had rather tell you than anyone else, because you are always indulgent, and you won't preach as papa would. He would forgive me in the end, I daresay, but he would begin by preaching—and I am so unhappy that I don't think I could bear a word."

"My dearest Gracie, *you* mean! *you* deceitful! I would not hear your enemy say so, and leave him unkicked. Nonsense, child," said the Colonel cheerily, laying his friendly hand upon Grace's shoulder. Her head was bent so that he could not see her face, and her tears were dropping into the rank grass and making the meadow a little more watery for the cows. "Stuff and nonsense, my dear. Some little girlish folly which you have concealed from Sir Allan, and which your own fancy has exaggerated into a matter of importance."

"It is not a little folly, Colonel. It is a big folly. I am engaged to be married—to a person whom my father has never seen—of whose very existence he is ignorant."

"Humph," exclaimed Stukely, "that sounds rather serious. But people get out of such engagements—occasionally."

"I shall never get out of mine," answered Grace with an heroic air. "I would die rather than break my word."

"Of course, of course," said the godfather soothingly.

"More especially as the person to whom I am engaged is very badly off, and not able to——"

"To maintain you," interjected the Colonel. "Naturally, my dear, naturally. That is an excellent reason for sticking to him. And now tell me all about it. When and where did you meet this gentleman?"

"In Paris, at the Louvre."

"The big shop for gowns, and bonnets, and things?"

"No, the picture gallery."

"Who introduced him to you?"

"Nobody. A mahlstick."

"A mahlstick introduced him?"

"Oh, godfather, please don't be shocked. I know how horrid it all was—how unladylike—how improper. I have thought about it and cried about it many a time since I came home. Nobody introduced him to me. You know how fond I am of painting. I worked very hard when I was in Paris; and I got permission from Madame Sartori to go and paint three times a week at the Louvre. Horrid old thing! I believe she was glad to get rid of me. She told off one of the governesses—a domestic drudge, a lady-help sort of person—to go with me, for which father paid five guineas a term extra. It was all very correct and proper so far. In fine weather we used to walk from Passy to the Louvre. In wet weather we had a *fiacre*, which I used to pay for out of my pocket money. Lady Darnel and father between them kept me very handsomely supplied."

"No doubt," said the Colonel, "and I have observed that 'Satan finds some mischief still,' as Dr. Watts says, for school boys and girls who have too much pocket money. Go on, Grace."

"One day I was copying a Madonna, by

Guido—not a bit like, I know, for my Madonna would come out with a purple complexion, like a cabman in cold weather. The picture was hung high, so I had to sit on a kind of platform four feet off the ground. It was very nice sitting up there and looking down at the people, and at the other students. There were three or four in the room. One of them was a remarkably handsome young man, who was copying a little Wouvermans, in water-colours, in a spirited, dashing style, which I thought wonderfully clever. He looked dreadfully ill, poor fellow!—such hollow cheeks—such a haggard look about his large dark eyes. But that naturally made him all the more interesting."

"Naturally," said the Colonel, "given a young man without sixpence and with a marked tendency to pulmonary consumption, and granted a generous-hearted girl, the result may be calculated upon as a certainty. Of course you fell in love with him on the spot."

"I am not that sort of person, Colonel. I don't suppose I should ever have given him a serious thought if it had not been for the accident which introduced us to each other. He talked a good deal to a frumpish little elderly woman who was toiling at a big altar-piece, and who looked as if she worked for her living. He had such bright, winning ways, that I could not help noticing him—a little. Mademoiselle Bouge, the governess, said he was the handsomest young man she had ever seen. One day I dropped my mahlstick."

"On purpose?"

"Oh, Colonel, how can you think so meanly of me? No, it was pure accident. He flew to pick it up. I thanked him—and then he lingered and began to talk."

"Was he a Frenchman?"

"A thorough Parisian. He told me, in the politest way, that my flesh tints were too blue, and gave me some excellent hints about colour. Then he went back to his easel, and took no further notice, except a particularly graceful bow when I left the room. When I went back two days afterwards he was there again, at another Wouvermans. He bowed when I went in; gentlemen bow first in France, you know; and I could not be so bearish as not to acknowledge his bow. I got on to my platform, and poor Mademoiselle Bouge sat on her usual bench, and stared at the pictures, in her usual way. My hand trembled so that I could hardly paint."

"And you dropped your mahlstick again."

"No, Colonel! How can you imagine such conduct? You have evidently a poor opinion of girls. I went on painting, wretchedly, for half an hour or so; getting that poor Madonna bluer and bluer with every touch of the brush; and just as I was beginning to despair of her, the young Frenchman came over to me, and asked me if I would allow him to give me a few more hints upon colouring, and harmony, and so on. I neither said yes nor no, only murmured vaguely, like a shy simpleton as I was. He seemed to think this gave him full permission, and he took the picture in hand, and told me how I had gone wrong and showed me what to do. This was the beginning of our friendship, which came about very gradually, almost unawares; but in a fortnight's time we were friends. We did not talk much. That would have been impossible in a public room, and under the eyes of Mademoiselle Bouge: but he used to contrive to give me a letter every time we met, and he was wonderfully clever at slipping the letter under my colour box, or into my hand, without poor old Bouge seeing him."

"He had done the same kind of thing very often before, no doubt."

"You ought not to say that, Colonel; it is not like your usual kindness. No, he told me, in his very first letter, that he had never been really in love before."

"They never have," muttered the Colonel.

"He wrote the loveliest letters."

"And you answered them?"

"I was obliged to answer *sometimes*. I hardly knew how wrong it was. You see I had been brought up in a place where I knew everybody, and I had no idea of being afraid of strangers. I told him who I was, and how I was finishing my education at Madame Sartori's; and he told me his own history, and that he was an orphan quite alone in the world, and that he belonged to a good old Burgundian family, and that he had come to Paris to study art."

"A regular Bohemian, no doubt."

"You ought not to say that, godfather. He always looked like a gentleman, though his clothes were shabby. And though he lived on the left side of the Seine, in the students' quarter, his manners were perfect."

"And his name. He had a name, I suppose."

"His name is Victor de Camillac," answered Grace, with dignity, "and I am engaged to him."

"Really and truly engaged to him? That is carrying things rather far with a young man with whom you only exchanged a few words about painting, and half-a-dozen surreptitious love letters."

"There were a great many more than half-a-dozen," answered Grace, "he wrote volumes. He gave me a letter every time I went to the Louvre—such clever letters, so eloquent, so poetical."

"I know the kind of thing. He is one of those men with whom letter-writing is a complaint," said the Colonel. "Your dragon, Miss Bouge, must have been a very sleepy personage to have had no suspicion of what was going on under her nose."

"Oh, she had her suspicions, poor soul, but I persuaded her to keep my secret. I blush to say that I appealed to her meanest instincts."

"As how?"

"You know the confectioner's at the corner of the Rue Castiglione?"

"No."

"Don't you? How I pity you. It is one of the best—I believe it is the best confectioner's in Paris. I used to take Bouge there every afternoon when I left the Louvre. 'Now, dear,' I used to say, 'take whatever you fancy,' and the poor soul used to revel in éclairs and choux and brioches, and méringues and red currant syrup, to an alarming extent."

"How she must have missed you when you left school," said the Colonel, laughing.

He could not bring himself to be very angry

with his god-daughter for this folly of hers; nor could he think very seriously of this interchange of love letters with a shabby-genteel Frenchman. The whole business seemed, at the first blush, too foolish for grave consideration; and yet, on reflection, Colonel Stukely told himself that it was a kind of folly which might entail disagreeable consequences. Very disagreeable if the young man were a scamp; and the circumstances favoured that inference.

"And do you mean to say, Gracie," he began, after a pause, "that you have engaged yourself, in black and white, to a man of whose surroundings and antecedents you knew absolutely nothing?"

"I knew everything," she answered indignantly. "Victor told me his whole history. He was thoroughly frank. He confessed that he had only just enough to live upon, poorly, and in a poor quarter. His father had been ruined by the Mexican war, having been tempted to put all his money into Mexican Bonds. When his father died Victor came to Paris to study art, in the hope of becoming a distinguished painter, like Meissonier or Vidal. If I would promise to marry him he told me he should have a new incentive to industry, perseverance, patience—the holiest and purest incentive."

"That fetched you," said the Colonel, "and you promised."

"Not for months after I received that letter. What a very feeble person you must think me, Colonel."

"I think you an adorable little goose," said her godfather.

"I don't think I should have consented to engage myself to him," pursued Grace, "only one day I missed him in the room where he and I had both been working."

"Still at your Guido?"

"Oh, no. I had gone into another room, and I was copying a flower piece. Victor advised me to paint flowers and fruit and things—dead nature, as he called them—rather than Italian Madonnas. One day he was missing, and the next time, and the next. I had not seen him for a week. I felt sure that he must be ill. I was very unhappy about him; haunted by the image of his poor pale face. At the end of the week he wrote to me, under cover to Mademoiselle Bouge, who brought me the letter to my room, with a fearful countenance, and told me it might have been the ruin of her to receive it, which was sheer nonsense, as even Madame Sartori's sharp eyes could not read the inside of a thick envelope."

"The letter told you he was dying, I presume," said the Colonel.

"It was only a few lines scribbled with a pencil, and written from what he thought would be his death-bed. It was a last adieu; for he told me that he had no hope of seeing me again."

"You did not go to see him, I hope," said the Colonel anxiously, not knowing to what compromising step the girl might have been tempted, in her inexperience of life.

"That would have been impossible. I think I might have persuaded that good old Bouge to ask for an evening out, and to go and see him for me. But there was no address to his letter. There never had been any address to his letters. My answers were to be sent to a Post Office in the Quartier Latin."

"A curious gentleman, to be ashamed to own where he lived," said the Colonel.

"It was only pardonable pride, poor fellow. He knew that my people were rich, and he was ashamed to let me know how shabby a street he lived in. As if that would make any difference to me!"

"You answered the death-bed letter?"

"Yes, godfather," Grace answered softly, hanging her pretty head, and contributing a few more tears to the watery meadow.

"And what kind of letter did you write, my dear?" asked the Colonel, gently.

"I'm afraid it was a very foolish one. I was so sorry for him, poor fellow—so sorry to think of his being alone, dying, in a wretched lodging—and I begged him to get well for my sake, and told him that I would be true to him in his poverty, and that if he would be content to wait for me till I could win my father's consent to our marriage, and be constant to me, as I would be to him, perhaps for years, I would give him the promise that he had so often pleaded for in those beautiful letters."

"I am very glad you made the matter contingent on your father's consent, my love," said the Colonel, cheerily. "The business is not half so bad as I thought. Was there anything more in your letter?"

"Only that if my father should refuse his consent to our engagement I would never marry anyone else. So far at least I was my own mistress. I might not be allowed to marry *him*, I loved my father too well to be disobedient or rebellious. But I pledged myself to be true to Victor even in life-long severance."

"Whew!" exclaimed the Colonel. "A pretty kettle of fish! And is that why you so unmercifully snubbed young Colchester, the Master of the Hounds, when we were out cub-hunting the other morning?"

"I am not aware that I snubbed Mr. Colchester," said Grace, blushing furiously.

"Oh, but he was aware of it. You treated him shamefully! Such a nice young fellow too, and so particularly attentive to you—opening gates and making way for you at fences, and lingering by your side to talk when he ought to have had no eyes except for those young hounds of his, till at last you drove him away by sheer incivility. When a man is Lord of the Manor and Master of the Hounds he hardly expects to be treated like that."

"I have nothing to do with Mr. Colchester's expectations," answered Grace, tossing up her head, but with tears still in the sweet hazel eyes. "It is cruel of you to talk like that, godfather, when I have told you that I am bound to poor Victor by a most sacred promise."

"Did you see much more of poor Victor after the death-bed betrothal?"

"We only met once after that, for my last term at Madame Sartori's was just coming to an end, and father and mother were coming to fetch me. Victor came to the Louvre on the very last day I painted there, looking like a ghost, poor fellow; and with a feverish light in his eyes. He ought not to have left his bed; but he was determined to see me before I went back to England. His poor hand trembled like a leaf when we shook hands. He thanked me with tears in his eyes for my letter, and implored me to keep my promise. He said he was prepared to wait a lifetime for me; but he hoped to overcome my father's objections to our marriage in a year or so, when he should have sold a few pictures and made a success in the Salon. 'Directly I have a little money and a shred of reputation I shall come to Darnel and ask for your hand boldly,' he said. I told him that my father was the most generous of men, and that I had plenty of money for both of us."

"And so you parted. And you have corresponded with him ever since, I conclude?"

"We have corresponded—at intervals. Victor writes the loveliest letters; but he is a very irregular correspondent. Sometimes a month goes by without my hearing from him, and I am tortured by the idea that he is ill or dying—dead, perhaps; while I am amusing myself playing tennis, and going to parties, in ignorance of his fate. And then comes a long eloquent letter, explaining his silence. He has been ill and out of spirits, too depressed to write, afraid to plague me with his misery—or he has been working at a picture like a demon, only to have it refused at the Salon."

"Not a cheerful correspondent," said the Colonel. "And now, Gracie, my pet, my darling, whom I can remember a chubby baby in a white frock and blue shoulder-knots, and with little blue shoes—how proud you were of those little shoes—now tell me, honestly, frankly, bravely, are you desperately in love with this young French painter, whose face your father has never seen?"

"I was very fond of him, Colonel, or I should never have given that promise."

"Of course not, but you have had a year and a half for sober reflection. A long time in such a young life as yours. And reflection has told you that you were very foolish to give such a promise, and you would be very glad to be released from it."

"For my father's sake," faltered Grace. "Yes, I should be glad to be free from that foolish engagement; for I am afraid it would grieve my dear father. And he is so good to me—so indulgent—every new kindness of his seems like a knife plunged into my heart."

"Well, my dear girl, you have two duties before you, painful, perhaps, both of them. First, to tell Sir Allan everything just as frankly as you have told me. Secondly, to write to Monsieur

Camillac, requesting him to release you from your promise."

"Oh, no, no, Colonel, don't ask me. I could not tell my father, and I could not ask Victor to release me—not now, when he is poor and ill and unhappy. If he were to become rich and admired, famous, I would not mind asking him to set me free."

"That is just like my generous, romantic Gracie," said the Colonel, smiling. "You would be true to a pauper and a failure; but you would ask for your freedom from a successful painter. Well, my child, you have trusted me, and I must prove myself worthy of your confidence. Take time to think of what I said just now. I feel sure that you will not be happy until you have made a full confession to your father, who would not scold you a whit more severely than I have done."

"But he would be so shocked, so grieved," exclaimed Grace. "I could not endure to see the grieved look in his face—his surprise in finding that I had kept a secret from him. He always praises me for my candour—and to find out all at once that I am a whited sepulchre. No, I could not bear it!"

"Better to pluck up your courage, Grace, and take the bull by the horns. A secret like yours cannot be kept for ever. This Monsieur Camillac is poor, an artist, and a Bohemian; and he knows that you are rich and will have an independent fortune under your mother's settlement when you come of age. I suppose you told him that."

"I told him all about myself and my people."

"Well, my dear child, can you suppose that a young man in his circumstances will be patient for ever, will hold his peace for ever, when he has the chance of marrying an heiress? Be sure that however quiet he may be now he will push his claims vigorously when you come of age. And that will be——"

"Next year," sighed Grace.

"Then, my love, the sooner you face your difficulties boldly the better it will be for your chances of happiness. Tell your father everything, while I am on the premises; and if my Grace wants any backer with the most indulgent of fathers, she knows she has a sturdy champion in her faithful old Colonel."

"Dear godfather, how good you are to me," murmured Grace, lifting up the soldier's sunburnt hand and kissing it.

"And now I think those ponies of yours must have had their mouths washed out and be ready for action," said the Colonel, who did not wish to press the sinner too hard just at first, trusting to Grace's own reflections to bring about the desired result.

They walked back to the carriage in silence, Grace was downcast; but the Colonel talked of indifferent matters in his pleasantest manner all the way home, and contrived to put his god-daughter into good spirits again before they reached Darnel Park.

Sir Allan rarely appeared at luncheon, and to-day Lady Darnel and he were both out. But Miss Darnel was always at her post. She was not locomotive; indeed she had a cat-like fondness for the house, rarely extending her peregrinations beyond a cat-like pacing to and fro of the terrace in front of the drawing-room windows, or a perambulation of the dewy lawns or shrubberies. She might be met at all times and seasons prowling about the corridors with that velvet footfall of hers. And thus it came about that nothing, not to the most attenuated particular of existence, could occur at Darnel without Dora's knowledge; hardly a sentence could be spoken of which she did not hear enough to divine the drift of the speaker. The servants had thus come to consider her omniscient, and to fear her accordingly. She was an admirable housekeeper, for her whole attention was riveted upon the details of existence at Darnel. She had no joys, no hopes, or fears—

no interests outside the Park gates. She was not without accomplishments, and she was not without intellectual culture—yet the world of politics, the world of art, the world of the past and of the future were to her a dead letter. She lived only to rule and reign in her little kingdom of Darnel. It may be conceived, therefore, what mental tortures she suffered on the occasion of her brother's second marriage, when she saw the sceptre slipping from her grasp.

"Has father driven to Scadleigh?" asked Grace, as she sat down to luncheon, looking very pretty in the dark grey cloth tailor gown, with a coquettish terra-cotta velvet waistcoat, just a touch of vivid colour to set off her milk-white skin, and harmonise with her ruddy brown hair.

"He has gone to London."

"To London?"

"Yes. He and Lady Darnel started directly you were gone. They drove off in a tremendous hurry to catch the express at Scadleigh."

"But father didn't say one word about it at breakfast," exclaimed Grace.

"I believe it was quite a sudden resolution. They are to be back to dinner. We are to dine at half-past eight, Colonel. I hope you won't mind."

"Not I," said the Colonel. "Grace and I will

sit in the firelight and tell each other fairy stories."

It was still that pleasant autumn season when evening fires are a luxury, and when home grows every day more homely.

"My father has gone to town on business, I suppose?" said Grace, sorely mystified by this unpremediated rush to London, which was so unlike her father's usual habits. "But why drag Lady Darnel with him?"

"I have not the faintest notion," said Dora. "Allan told me nothing beyond the bare fact that he was going to take Lady Darnel to town, and that they would be back to dinner. He begged me to convey his apologies to you, Colonel Stukely."

"There was no occasion for apologies," said the Colonel.

Both he and Grace knew Miss Darnell well enough to be convinced that she knew all about her brother's business in London. Those sharp ears, those acute perceptions of hers were rarely at fault.

Sir Allan's business in London did not remain long a mystery to his trusted friend. When the ladies had left the dining-room that evening the two old comrades in arms drew their chairs to the hearth, and lighted their cigarettes, and then came the hour of confidence.

"I daresay you all wondered what took us up to town in such a hurry this morning," said Allan.

"Grace has an active imagination, and she exercised it vigorously between luncheon and five o'clock tea," answered the Colonel, laughing; "but my sluggish old brain has not been much disturbed by the mystery. People think nothing of an eighty mile journey to and fro by express. It would have been different if you had had to go in a dhak."

"I took Clara to see Sir Clarkson Andrews."

"Indeed."

"Yes, I have been anxious about her for a long time; and in spite of our family doctor's assurance that there was no cause for alarm, I determined to consult an experienced physician. So, as this morning was particularly fine, and I had no work to do at home, I persuaded her to go to Cavendish Square with me. I telegraphed for an appointment from Scadleigh, so there was no time lost. Sir Clarkson was kindness itself, had a long talk with my wife, assured me that there was nothing organically wrong, only a tendency to languor and low spirits, which might develope into something worse if we were not careful. He strongly recommended me to take Lady Darnel to Italy for the winter. I am to move her from place to place, give her plenty of change of scene; in a word, to do all in my power to amuse and interest her. 'I have no doubt Darnel Park is a charming place; but frankly now, Sir Allan, isn't it just a little dull?' he asked. I admitted the fact. 'Of course, all parks are dull,' he said 'shut in from the outside world—a dignified seclusion. Very few neighbours within easy reach, I daresay.' 'Very few whom Lady Darnel cares for,' replied I. 'Just so,' said Sir Clarkson. 'Oh, I know those parks. They have to answer for shortening the lives of our aristocracy. Take Lady Darnel along the Riviera, letting her see every place that is worth seeing, and then drop quietly down into Italy for the winter. You can take her back to Darnel when the primroses are in bloom; and I pledge my honour she will be a new creature!'"

"Well, my dear Allan, this was rather cheering than otherwise."

"It was comforting to know what is wrong. Poor dear Clare, I do not think it is the dulness of Darnel Park she has felt half so much as the want of sociability upon the part of my old county friends. *That* has wounded her deeply."

"Have they been more unsociable than county people usually are?" asked the Colonel, with pardonable hypocrisy.

He was very well aware of the fact, both from Miss Darnel's innuendoes and from his own personal observation. The county had given Sir Allan's second wife the coldest reception compatible with civility.

"They are not absolutely uncivil; they would not dare be that to my wife," said Allan, "but they have not been cordial. There has been no real friendliness. They take every occasion to let my wife feel that she is not in their own particular set; and she does feel it, more, I believe, for my own sake than her own. She is too proud to court anybody's friendship. The people all made their duty calls when we came home from our honeymoon; but there was a flavour of duty about the thing which was unpleasant. Then came three or four state dinners to which my wife went, and where she was made to feel somehow by the feminine portion of the party that she was received on sufferance. We gave two or three dinners that winter, at which some of my old friends were present: but there was a suspicious number of previous engagements, and I know poor Clare felt humiliated at finding it such a difficult matter to make up a party of twenty. Since then we have fallen into the way of living almost entirely alone. The Rector and his wife come to us in a friendly way, very often, as you have seen. Occasionally I have an old army friend down from London. Young Colchester drops into luncheon now and then in the hunting season—and that is about all. Clare never complains, and she is not dependent for her happiness upon society: but I know she feels the slight which is involved for a woman in her position in not being sought out and made much of. In fact," said Sir Allan, waxing savage, as was his wont when he touched on this topic, "I shall be very glad to get Lady Darnel away from this accursed hole."

"Grace will go with you, of course," observed the Colonel.

"I had not been thinking of her."

"My dear Allan, she would eat her heart out if you left her alone with Miss Darnel."

"Those two do not get on well together, certainly. And Grace adores my wife. Yet it seems a pity to take her away just at the beginning of the fox-hunting, and after I have bought her that new mare. Grace is so fond of hunting; and young Ted Colchester——

"Is so fond of Grace. Is that what you were going to say?"

"It is 'pretty near the truth, I think. And Colchester is a thoroughly good fellow, the only man in the neighbourhood who has shown himself staunch and cordial since my marriage. He belongs to a good old family, and he has a fine estate. I should be proud of such a son-in-law."

"And you may have him for a son-in-law, if you play your cards properly. Take an old bachelor's advice, Allan. I don't think Gracie cares much for Edward Colchester now. He has been too attentive, too devoted, is too obviously a good match. The first idea of a high-spirited romantic girl like Grace is generally to throw herself away upon a pauper. If Colchester were a penniless nobody, and could only approach her by stealth, I have no doubt she would adore him. But as he is well off, and you have broadly hinted that you would like her to marry him, the natural result is that she despises him. Take her to Italy with you, keep her closely under Lady Darnel's eye, and when she comes back to Darnel the odds are she will like young Colchester ever so much better than when she went away. She has seen hardly any other eligible young man for the last year and a half, and he has palled upon her in consequence. Distance will lend enchantment to the view."

"What an old fox you are, Weldon," said Sir Allan, smiling. "Yes, I believe you are right. Grace shall go with us, even if the new mare and old Blackie have to eat their heads off while she is away. Perhaps you'll winter at Darnel, and keep the stud in good working order for us."

"You are too good, my dear fellow," replied the Colonel, inwardly shuttering at the idea of a winter spent with Dora. "No, I shall stay in town, if I fail in finding a place down here; and after nearly two months I am as far from realising my ideal hunting box as I was when I first came."

In the drawing-room that evening Sir Allan was in unsually good spirits. The idea of getting his wife away from Darnel for a good long time was a relief to him. In spite of his perfect happiness in his married life there were times when he felt the chilling attitude which some of his oldest acquaintances had assumed since his second marriage. Up to that time he had deemed these people his friends; and now they had been tested he knew they had never been more than acquaintances. Time had not made them loyal and true. Yes, it was delightful to think of being in a foreign land with his beloved wife, amidst strange faces. He felt grateful to Sir Clarkson for having insisted upon Italy. He talked of nothing but their journey.

"Grace, you are to go with us," he said. "Your godfather there has promised and vowed for you, that you will be very good, and give us no trouble, and that you will help me to take care of Clare. So you will have to 'settle your fine joints,' as old Capulet says, get all your frocks and furbelows ready, at a very short notice."

"How good of you, dear father."

"You like to go, then?" said Sir Allan, looking at her sharply. "You don't mind missing the hunting?"

Gracie blushed at the question, as if it touched a sensitive chord.

"One can have fox-hunting any year," she said, "but not an Italian tour."

"And your Parisian French will be useful to me when Clare is not at my side," said Sir Allan. "I used to spout Racine when I was a boy, and I can read a French novel; but I can never hit upon little common phrases when I am in a hurry. You will have to be ready in less than a week, Grace; for as soon as ever I can put my affairs in decent order we will be off. Clare is such an orderly person that she is always ready."

"I have nothing to do but to be orderly," said Lady Darnel, smiling at him. "Dora takes all household cares off my hands, and you never exact anything from me."

"Yes, I do, my dear. I look to you for the

happiness of my life, and you have never disappointed me," answered Sir Allan tenderly. "Well, we will start directly I have paid the quarter's accounts, and made things straight with the steward. I dropped in at the bank as we drove to the station and got four hundred in notes, to begin the war."

"Just as Bismarck called in all the gold he could get before he challenged Austria," said the Colonel.

"I used to carry circular notes, but I have found of late years that your British bank note will pass current in most parts of the Continent. And I treated myself to a brace of revolvers at Lancaster's—the last refinement in travelling pistols."

"Prudent man!" exclaimed the Colonel. "You will be quite disappointed if there is no encounter with brigands to bring your firearms into active service."

"Grace," said the Colonel, turning to his god-daughter. "If you really mean cub-hunting to-morrow you had better go to bed. It is nearly eleven."

"Of course I mean cub-hunting. Do you think I would lose a run now that I am to be away all the season? But it hardly seems worth while going to bed when one is to get up again at four o'clock. Good-night, father, and thank you so much for taking me to Italy. It is the dream of my life."

"It has been the dream of my life," said her aunt, without looking up from her work-basket, "but a dream which will never be realised."

This was just one of those speeches which make everyone feel uncomfortable, and for which there seems to be no appropriate answer. It was the signal for a general departure.

Sir Allan, Colonel Stukely, and Grace were in the saddle before five o'clock next morning, and away over the dewy uplands, and in and out of dripping copses, before six. Grace's new mare behaved beautifully, carried her young mistress as if she had been a feather-weight, and evidently revelled in her work. Sir Allan took his line; Grace had her own ideas, and the Colonel, who was not so familiar with the country, stuck close to Grace, admiring her pretty figure and her dashing horsemanship, and altogether very proud of his god-daughter.

Mr. Colchester was as devoted as a Master of Hounds can be, and a keen observer would have been amused to see the struggle between duty and inclination which tore at his heart-strings every time he had to leave Grace's side in order to direct the instincts of his young hounds. He seemed happiest when the pack were in full cry and he and Grace were galloping side by side across country. Then there were gates to be opened, hedges to be taken first by his heavy hunter, so as to leave a safer jump for Grace, who naturally scorned such old-womanish attentions, infinitely preferring to have led the way over the most breakneck point in the fence.

Colonel Stukely kept close to these two all the time, admiring Grace's admirer almost as heartily as he admired Grace herself. And, indeed, Squire Colchester, in his grey coat and black velvet cap, was as pleasing a specimen of a young English landowner as anybody could desire to see; tall, broad-shouldered, fair complexioned, with cheery blue eyes, and crisp brown hair, which would have curled all over his head had it not been kept closely shorn. It was a frank, kindly face, characteristic of the man, who was good-nature personified; but the firmly-moulded lips and square chin told of a resolute temper and a strong will.

It was in the course of a second run that an incident occurred which had a startling effect upon Grace and the Colonel. They were crossing a common within three miles of Darnel Park, a picturesque common on the crest of a hill, all hillock and hollow, crowned with a cluster of old

Scotch firs. As they galloped over the rugged, uneven ground, a little recklessly on Grace's part, Juno, the new mare, gave a desperate shy, for the first time since her mistress had ridden her, and Grace looked round to see the cause of her alarm.

A man was lying against a sandy hillock, half-buried in the furze—a slender figure, in an old velveteen coat, travel-stained, out-at-elbows, a dark head half hidden in a soft felt hat.

As Grace turned to look at him the man raised himself slowly from his recumbent position, and looked round him listlessly, vaguely, as if suddenly awakened, but not in the direction of the young horsewoman, who was some paces away from the hillock where he sat. Still looking back at him, she gave a faint half-stifled cry, just as young Colchester came galloping across the common, almost brushing against the man on the hillock, and bore Grace and the Colonel along with him, as on the wings of a whirlwind.

"They're running like old boots in the copse," he cried, pointing with his whip.

"Godfather," gasped Grace, trying to hold her horse back as they were galloping along a lane, so as not to be heard by the Master, "did you see that man on the common?"

"The tramp who startled your horse. Yes, I saw him."

"He is not a tramp. He is Victor de Camillac. Oh, how ill and wretched he looked. I should have stopped if that horrid man hadn't come rushing by. Do go back to him. Ask him where he is stopping—why he has come here? Do, Colonel, for my sake. And have you any money about you?"

"Two or three pounds, perhaps."

"Give him all you have, please, for me. He looked so poor."

"Come along, Miss Darnel," shouted Mr. Colchester; "they've got him."

And Grace cantered after him with a little hypocritical laugh, pretending to be delighted at the idea of bloodshed, although she always felt ready to cry at this stage of the entertainment, and told herself that it was too bad, and that she would never hunt again; and then, with a charming inconsistency, came out next day.

"The devil," muttered the Colonel, as he rode slowly up the hill, "here's a pretty kettle of fish."

It was the same classical expression which he had made use of yesterday, when Grace told him the story of her engagement, and with the Colonel it meant a great deal.

This man's presence within an hour's walk of Darnel foreboded mischief. His disreputable appearance indicated a lapse into the lowest depths of poverty. And what generosity or forbearance could be expected from a destitute adventurer? The man held Grace's promise of marriage, under her own hand. Could it be supposed that he would not make it an instrument of torture, unless he were bought off, and got rid of somehow. He was here in the girl's own neighbourhood; he would discover the position her father occupied; he would perhaps be told of Edward Colchester's devotion to her, of the general expectation that she would marry him. These things are always village gossip, long before the principals themselves have made up their minds. If this adventurer were to show Grace's letters to Edward Colchester, her future would be blighted, her father's hopes cheated. It was a detestable entanglement. The Colonel could not help feeling angry with Grace as he rode up the hill. To think that a girl could so trifle with fate, out of sheer silliness—could so forfeit self-respect, endanger her reputation—bring pain and discredit upon her parents.

"The only hope is, that if the man is poor, we may be able to buy him pretty cheap," thought the Colonel.

CHAPTER III.

KEEPING HIM AT BAY.

COLONEL STUKELY rode slowly along the top of the ridge, looking for the sandy hillock, to leeward of that cluster of rugged firs, where Grace and he had seen the vagabond lying. He found that particular hillock easily enough; there were the prints of the horses' hoofs to show him the way; but the man was gone. He rode all over the common, round and about, looking for him, almost as closely as the hounds would have hunted for a fox; but there was no sign of a human creature sheltering behind any of those furze bushes, or in any of those hollows.

He heard the hounds winding round the base of the hill, and went zig-zagging down to find Grace in a field at the bottom. The fox had gone to ground, and the huntsmen were getting the hounds together to go back to the kennels, digging out not being counted as a virtue in this district. Mr. Colchester was in high spirits, his young hounds had worked admirably, and he had been with Grace almost all the morning. It was only nine o'clock now, they would be back in time for a latish breakfast. Grace and her father had dismounted, and were standing side by side, while the grooms eased the saddles. Grace gave a little appealing look at the Colonel, which he answered by a grave shake of his head.

"You'll come to breakfast with us, Colchester," said Sir Allan, "we are nearer than the Manor. And it may be the last time we shall breakfast together for five or six months."

"The last time," gasped Colchester. "What do you mean?"

"Lady Darnel is ordered to the south for the winter, and we are all off, as soon as ever we can start."

"All! You and Lady Darnel, I suppose."

"And Grace. Grace is going with us."

"What, you are going to lose the hunting, just when Sir Allan has bought you that perfect mare, and with poor old Blackbird as fit as a fiddle, too. How *can* you, Miss Darnel."

"Yes, it's very sad, isn't it?" murmured Grace when she was in her saddle again, and they were jogging homewards.

She hardly knew what she was saying, her mind was so full of that figure lying against the heathy knoll, that rusty velveteen jacket, that battered old felt wide-awake, the very image of destitution and decay. And that vagabond was her lover, her plighted lover, the man for whose sake she had renounced all the rest of mankind, binding herself by a life-long vow. And then she glanced shyly at the master of the hounds, trotting beside her along the rustic lane, the frank manly face, the bright English complexion, the look of gentle blood, the clear outlook of eyes which had never feared the face of a foe; and she knew in her heart of hearts that this man cared for her above all women.

"Are you really going?" he asked ruefully.

"Really and truly," she said, "but it is not for so very long. We shall come back in the spring, as soon as the weather is mild enough for Lady Darnel."

"Not before May," said Sir Allan. "Our climate is not to be trusted before May."

"And May is about the most treacherous month in the year," interjected the Colonel. "Never put your trust in May. All the old English saws tell you that."

"And you are going to Italy," said Edward Colchester, growing more and more despondent; "and there are these cursed hounds to tie a fellow by the leg. What part are you going to?"

He had not been much of a continental traveller, a fortnight in Paris being his largest idea in that line. He had boasted that Scotland

and Ireland were good enough for his holiday ground. Why go to Norway to fish for salmon, when one could have better fishing in Connemara, among a people who spoke one's mother tongue more or less? Edward Colchester had the sturdy, true blue British temperament, and thought that if God had given him a fortune it was his duty to spend it in his own country. And he did spend liberally in the place where he was born. The manor was maintained in noble style, chiefly for the advantage of three maiden aunts, his own habits being of the simplest. The bulk of the expenses of the kennels fell upon him; for although ostensibly a subscription pack, the Wilton Moor hounds must have gone on very short commons, and the Wilton Moor huntsmen must have ridden very sorry cattle, had they depended on the liberality of the neighbourhood.

"What part of Italy?" inquired Mr. Colchester, as he jogged along by Grace's side.

"I think father said we were to go to the lakes?"

"Como and that kind of thing. Ah, very nice, I daresay. Any salmon, I wonder? Well, Miss Darnel, as I have never seen Italy, I'll run over and join you for a fortnight or so in April, if Sir Allan will let me!"

"You would find it very dull, I am afraid," replied Grace sadly. "We are not going for sight-seeing or gaiety; but solely on account of Lady Darnel's health."

"I shouldn't care how quiet you might be. I should go to see Italy—and you."

"I say, Colchester, where did you get that chestnut the whip rode this morning?" asked Sir Allan, and the master was obliged to leave Grace's side and talk to her father.

Grace fell back directly, and began to question the Colonel.

"How dreadful!" she said, when he had told her of his failure. "If he should go away from the neighbourhood without help. Penniless, starving, perhaps."

"No fear of that, I think. You may depend he has come to this neighbourhood meaning to get help, and from you. Poor Grace! You'll hear of him soon enough, be sure. But whenever he does approach you, mind you refer him to me."

"How unkindly you speak of him, Colonel, as if he were my enemy."

"How can I think of him except as your enemy. A penniless adventurer who inveigles a school girl into an engagement which he must know she can only keep at the sacrifice of her prospects in life."

"He did not inveigle me. I was very foolish, perhaps, but I acted of my own free will. And you have no right to call him an adventurer, just because he is poor, and because you see him for the first time under very humiliating circumstances," said Grace, plucking her handkerchief out of the pigskin to dry a sudden rush of tears.

"I do not believe that any industrious, well-meaning young man would fall so low, Grace. There is a providence for struggling youth; and when a young fellow drops below the level of his own class be sure there is generally a good reason for the fall. You saw this fellow in Paris painting for a livelihood. You say he has the education of a gentleman, and that he paints well. Such a man has no right to be lying on Chicksand Common dressed like a tramp."

"It may be a disguise," said Grace, more and more indignant; "besides, you ought to remember that it is sometimes more difficult for a gentleman to keep his head above water than for an agricultural labourer or a mechanic. Somebody says that the high roads in Australia are made and mended by men who have taken honours at Oxford and Cambridge. Education is a drug in the market everywhere."

"The young man looks disreputable and dissipated."

"He looks very ill," said Grace.

"If he comes to Darnel this afternoon you had better take him straight to the drawing-room and introduce him to Sir Allan as your affianced husband, since you are so confident about him," retorted the Colonel, getting angry.

"Which means that you wash your hands of me and my troubles," said Grace, piteously.

"It means that I will help you, if I possibly can. But I will not encourage you in a folly—a mistaken sense of honour and self sacrifice. I love you so well, Grace, that if I thought this man were worthy of you, granting him to be a pauper, and if I knew your heart was set upon marrying him, I would use my strongest endeavours to reconcile your father to a bad match. But I have a shrewd suspicion that the man is a scamp and a scoundrel; and I am very sure that in your heart of hearts you don't care a straw for him. So I shall make it my business to arrange matters civilly and liberally with the gentleman. And if you are only good and submissive, I believe I shall be able to tell you in a week that you are as free as air."

"Dear—dearest Colonel!" cried Grace, forgetting herself. "But you will not behave unkindly to poor Victor."

"I mean to treat him very handsomely. I will

give him a fair start, with a nice little sum in hand in a new country, at a considerable distance from Darnel Park."

"But that will take a heap of money."

"The money shall be forthcoming. You and I can square accounts when you are of age."

"My best of friends."

"And when all is settled, and your Parisian friend has returned you those foolish letters, you can go to Sir Allan and tell him all about it very quietly. And then your mind will be at ease ever afterwards."

"It will be dreadful to tell papa," said Grace ruefully. "He will preach me *such* a sermon."

"Even a sermon may be endured from so good a father," replied the Colonel, with his kindly smile, "and, after all, sermons are good things in their way."

"Yes, I will tell him all, godfather, when Victor has released me from my promise; and if he should send me a letter, or come to the house, which he could hardly do, poor fellow, in that dreadful coat, I will let you know directly."

They put their horses at a trot, and followed Sir Allan and young Colchester, who had got a good start of them by this time, and there was no more confidential talk between Grace and her godfather.

The dining-room at Darnel looked a delightful place after a morning in dewy fields and damp copses, on breezy commons, and over wide uplands. The old hearth, with its dog-stove and brass furniture, the hissing urn, the loaded sideboard, the table bright with chrysanthemums and scarlet geraniums, and the fine old Swansea breakfast service—everything looked inviting—while the mistress of the house, in her neat, olive-green cashmere gown and linen collar, was the most charming object in the room. Lady Darnel was not one of those picturesque matrons who come to breakfast in a flowing satin robe, trimmed with ostrich plumage. She had not yet risen to that loose and shapeless splendour of attire which takes its inspiration from Japanese screens, and finds its material in Oriental bazaars. Neat and trim, and thoroughly English, she smiled upon her husband in a gown which might have cost from two to three pounds.

Those plain toilets only vexed Dora Darnel, who had secret yearnings for the Japanese, and had not courage to indulge them in the face of Lady Darnel's simplicity. Her mind was also exercised as to what Lady Darnel did with her pin money, which was large. She certainly did not spend it on dress, and if she disposed of it in works of charity, she was verily and indeed one of those excellent Christians whose left hand knows not what the right hand gives.

Dora had discussed this subject many a time and oft with her particular friends, those people who had held themselves a little aloof from Lady Darnel, but who still cultivated Sir Allan's incomparable sister.

"My conviction is that Lady Darnel is making a purse," she would conclude solemnly, as if it were altogether iniquitous to make purses.

"But why, my dear Dora, why should she do that, when you tell me Sir Allan has provided handsomely for her in the event of his death?" asked her friend.

"*Most* handsomely," said Dora. "But for all that I believe she is making a purse. Some women are born misers."

Clare Darnel had not the air of a woman of miserly soul as she sat at the head of the table this morning dispensing tea and coffee, and smiling upon her adoring husband, who had seated himself by her side. She looked brighter and happier than she had looked for a long time. The prospect of escape from her narrow surroundings, the idea of travelling with the man she tenderly loved, among new and beautiful scenes, was full of delight. She was not a weak woman, and she had met the coldness of her husband's old acquaintances with a quiet scorn. She despised them for misjudging her—despised them for their inability to accept her for her own sake, for their petty prejudices and suspicions. She knew that she might have been one of the worst women in England, her sins only falling short of law-court exposure; and yet if she had come to Darnel Park as the daughter of a great house, a personage, the county would have opened its arms to receive her. But she came to Darnel as a nobody, and all manner of evil was suspected about her. She had borne her isolation without a murmur, for she was a woman of infinite resources, and was in no wise dependent upon society for amusement or happiness; but she had been deeply grieved by the knowledge of her husband's pain at the unfriendliness of those whom he had counted as his friends.

And to turn her back upon this trouble, to go among strangers and strange scenery, to escape from those cold critical glances of Dora Darnel's, this was indeed delight; such delight that the thought of it made her for the moment forgetful of a deeper, darker trouble which had been weighing her to the ground of late, the one heavy burden of her life, a burden that she had set herself to endure in secret.

That breakfast after the cub hunting was a most

genial meal. Edward Colchester was as hungry as the proverbial hunter, and eat and talked with a most cheerful clatter, his talk naturally being a recapitulation of the morning's work, and of other mornings; what they had done and what they ought not to have done; whether one particular fox was the hunted fox, or a new fox—a point nicely debated, as exemplified by the conduct of said fox, between Mr. Colchester and the Colonel. Even Grace brightened and joined in the conversation, and showed herself wonderfully *au fait* as to the little ways and devices of old dog foxes, and the haunts and manners of cubs.

"You have such eyes," exclaimed Colchester, rapturously, "I believe you know every earth within thirty miles."

"I ride and drive about a good deal, and one cannot help using one's eyes," said Grace modestly.

"I know you have helped me to find some of our best foxes," replied Colchester. "By-the-bye, there is foxhunting somewhere near Rome, isn't there?"

"In the Campagna," suggested the Colonel.

"Well, now if their season only began after ours was over I might meet you at Rome, Sir Allan, and we might have some sport in the Campagna, eh?" asked Colchester.

"It would be delightful. But I'm afraid an Italian April would be too warm for hunting."

"By Jove, we have some deuced hot days here before we leave off," said Colchester. "But hunting or no hunting, I shall join you in the spring, if you'll have me."

"We shall be charmed to have you," said Lady Darnel.

"Quite a family party," sneered Dora.

She was just young enough to be jealous of her niece's superior youth and prettiness. She had had her own chances and had thrown them away, because they were not up to the level of her expectations; and now it galled her to see the Lord of the Manor at Grace's feet, and to see Grace dallying with her conquest.

"I daresay she thinks him hardly good enough for her," she thought. "She expects some nobleman to fall in love with her wasp waist and her reckless riding."

Edward Colchester lingered till nearly luncheon time. He went to the stables with Sir Allan while Grace was changing her dress, and there was that general overhauling of horseflesh which seems a source of perennial delight, even to the grooms and lads who have to bear the heat and burden of bringing the animals out and trotting them up and down. And when the stable inspection was over, Grace was discovered on the terrace in front of the drawing-room, all bloom and freshness in her pretty walking gown; and at Mr. Colchester's request she took him to see the conservatories, and that superb collection of chrysanthemums which was the autumnal glory of Darnel Park.

"You'll come too, won't you, auntie?" said Grace, appealingly.

It was but rarely she called Dora "auntie," and the unwonted tenderness seemed like a cry of distress. She would have done almost anything to escape a *tête-à-tête* with the master of the hounds; she who was audacity itself in the field when she trotted up to him to give him little wrinkles as to the whereabouts of foxes.

So Dora went the round of the glass houses, and explained the chrysanthemums to Edward Colchester, who found himself called upon to be interested in the different breeds, and rapturous about the Japanese varieties, and attentive to Dora Darnel at every point. It was altogether a disappointing business, and he fell into fearful yawnings before he had done.

"You seem dreadfully sleepy," said Dora.

"I was at the kennels at a quarter to four," he murmured, apologetically.

"And you are dying to go home for a nap,"

said Dora. "We won't look at any more flowers to-day."

"Oh, yes, let me see them all," pleaded Colchester, clinging to a straw, still faintly hoping for a few words alone with Grace.

But there was no detaching Grace from her aunt, and although young Colchester stayed till the luncheon gong sounded, he had to leave at last without having spoken those few words. But it would be in his power to make another opportunity before Sir Allan carried his daughter off to the south, if he had made up his mind to speak those words.

CHAPTER IV.

"LIFE-STIFLING FEAR, SOUL-STIFLING SHAME."

GRACE spent the day in apprehension, expecting some sign from her betrothed—a letter delivered secretly—a messenger asking to see her—some token that he was near at hand, and had come to that neighbourhood on her account. As the day wore on without bringing any such token, her fears and perplexities increased rather than diminished. She thought that he was lying somewhere; under a hedge, or to leeward of a haystack perhaps; too ill, too weak to crawl to a better shelter; helpless, penniless, friendless, sick and dying; while she who had sworn to love and cherish him was lolling in a luxurious easy chair, beside the bright hearth in her dainty little den, surrounded by hothouse flowers, and new books, and an Erard piano, and all the best and prettiest things that money can buy. Her generous tender heart, the heart which grieved even for slaughtered foxes, was sorely tortured by the picture of his destitution, by the bitter contrast between her fate and his. It was not because she loved him that she was so sad for his sake. She no longer loved him. That foolish, romantic fancy of hers, born of the idleness of a schoolgirl's life in a strange land, that childish dream had died long ago. For nearly a year past that secret engagement had been a terror and burden for her. She had longed ardently for some way of escape. She prayed that her godfather might succeed in undoing the knot she had tied for herself. Yet she could not put away the vision of that pale face, those haggard eyes and hollow cheeks; a face which to her troubled imagination seemed like the image of death itself.

All through the long afternoon she sat in her own room expectant, anxious, much too anxious to employ herself in any way, trembling at every footstep in the corridor, lest it should announce a messenger from Camillac. Five, six, seven o'clock struck from her little timepiece, and still there was no news. She had not gone down to afternoon tea, shrinking from the sight of her father and Lady Darnel; but she knew that she must go down to dinner, or else excite everybody's wonder. She was not the kind of girl to take to her bed after an early run with the hounds. So she dressed and went down to the drawing-room, and went in to dinner with the rest of the family, and sat in torture all dinner-time, expecting every time a footman approached her with a vegetable dish that he was coming to deliver some mysterious message. But the dinner came to an end, and no such message reached her.

Sir Allan began to yawn directly they got back to the drawing-room. He had been up to London and back the day before—he had been in the saddle at half-past four that morning. The Colonel and Grace yawned in concert. It was a chorus of stifled yawns.

"If you hunting people are so sleepy you had really better go to bed," exclaimed Dora, irritably.

She was one of those objectionable persons who are never sleepy. She was in the habit of playing classical music to the family of an evening, and liked her people to listen and admire.

"Dora is right," said Sir Allan, "I am only a nuisance here, so I'll say good night."

The Colonel and Grace followed suit. Lady Darnel said she had some letters to write, and would go to her own room to write them. She knew that even when he was sleeping her husband liked her to be near him; and her pretty morning-room adjoined his bedroom.

"You won't mind my deserting you, will you, Dora?" she asked sweetly, knowing that Miss Darnel detested early hours.

Dora replied in her blandest tones. She could amuse herself for an hour or two with Beethoven, if the noise of the piano would not disturb them upstairs.

"We shall not hear it, but it would be very nice if we did," said Lady Darnel.

They all went away, and Dora had the spacious drawing-room all to herself. It was brightened by a glowing fire of coal and logs, and by the light of lamps under coloured shades, and it was beautified by masses of hot-house bloom in great majolica jars of blue and yellow, and dull Indian red. It was in all respects as delightful a room as the heart of woman could desire: and yet its spaciousness gave an idea of desolation and abandonment when only one person was left in occupation.

Dora began a rondo of Beethoven's, but she played listlessly, without fire, without expression; and before she had played three pages her fingers were lying idle on the keys as the player sank into a deep reverie.

She was roused from her thoughtful abstraction by a sound on the terrace outside—a sound that seemed like the tread of feet upon the gravel. She ran to one of the windows and lifted the edge of the blind, and looked out into the darkness, with her face close against the glass. The night was pitchy dark. She could see nothing.

Then she opened the casement, and listened intently for some minutes, but there was no recurrence of the sound which had startled her.

Still she was not satisfied. She rang for a servant, and told him to go out upon the terrace and see if there was anyone lurking about.

"I certainly heard footsteps," she said, "about ten minutes ago."

The footman had a faintly incredulous air, though he was too well bred to express his unbelief. He went into the hall, slowly and laboriously withdrew the bolts of the great door, strolled out upon the terrace, and walked about three yards in each direction. The night was so dark that a regiment might have been in ambush at either end of the terrace, and the footman would have been none the wiser. He came back to the drawing-room and assured Miss Darnel that there was not a mortal on the terrace or in the Italian garden; and then he went back to the servants' hall and enlarged upon Miss Darnel's fidgetty, prying ways and love of late hours, while he finished his supper.

"I suppose she'll keep me hanging about till half after eleven before I can take those lamps away," he grumbled.

It was nearly eleven, and Sir Allan had not yet gone to bed. He had taken off his coat and put on a loose velvet jacket, and was smoking a cigarette in his wife's morning-room. He always enjoyed being alone with her, always had something particular to say to her, some scheme or arrangement to discuss. He never knew weariness in her society; and even to-night, tired as he was, he was loth to go to bed without the customary talk.

Since yesterday his mind had been full of the Italian trip.

"And you are glad to go away with me?" he said.

"Very, very glad. More glad than I can say."

"In that case you ought not to have waited for the doctor's orders. Directly you felt a yearning for change of scene you ought to have told me to take you away."

"I could not be so selfish, Allan, knowing how fond you are of Darnel."

"I am fond of no place in which you are not happy."

"I have been very happy here—with you."

"Yes, you *have been*—at first, perhaps. You were happy here, and so was I—completely happy in the beginning of a new life. But you have not been happy lately, Clare. There has been something weighing on your mind; and I have a shrewd suspicion that it is the polar atmosphere of Darnel that has been freezing my darling's tender heart."

"Oh, Allan, how can you think me so weak. What other society can I want when I have you?"

But Sir Allan had made up his mind upon the subject.

"Women are sensitive upon small matters," he said. "Never mind, my dear. We shall be far away from the people who have slighted you next week, beside the tideless waters of the Mediterranean. The money is ready there in the cabinet—four hundred in circular notes, and we can have plenty more when that is spent. Our Italian tour will be like a second honeymoon; and it shall be a long honeymoon."

He opened the cabinet while he was talking, and pulled out a drawer inside. It was an old

Italian cabinet in ebony and ivory, full of curious little drawers and recesses. From one of the drawers Sir Allan took out a bundle of bank notes, and looked at them and fingered them like a child with a new toy, longing to be off and away, scattering those notes in hotels and in smart little shops at gay continental watering-places. He meant this journey with his second wife to be one of delight for them both—for her the delight of strange places and lovely scenery; for him the rapture of seeing her happiness. He had written to an old club-house chum to secure a good courier. Lady Darnel would take her maid, and he his faithful old valet. Grace was young enough to shift for herself.

He put the notes back into the open drawer, and took the revolvers from one of the recesses. They were packed in a neat little Russia-leather case. He opened it and took out the pistols, and descanted upon their beauty.

"They are the prettiest things I have seen for an age," he said.

"I hope you may have no occasion to use them, Allan," answered his wife, averting her eyes with a look of fear.

"You don't like to see them in my hand?"

"I have a horror of all firearms."

"My dearest, I forgot," he cried, putting the

revolver which he had been examining back into its case.

He felt angry with himself for talking of the wretched thing, remembering that dark chapter in Clare's life in which a gun had done such dreadful work.

His cigarette was finished by this time. He bent down to kiss his wife as she sat at the writing-table.

"You will not stay up too late, dear?" he said.

"No, I have only a couple of letters to write—one to the dear old vicar to tell him of our change of plan. He was to have come to us for a week before Christmas, don't you know?"

"Of course. He must come to us next May."

He went to the bedroom which opened out of this sanctum of Lady Darnel's, and left his wife bending over her desk, in the light of the reading lamp. There was a large fire in the old-fashioned basket grate, such a fire as a well-trained servant always makes on a mild evening, as if it were required to roast an ox, or at least, a baron of beef. On coming into the room just now Lady Darnel's first impulse had been to open one of the windows. They were French casement windows opening on to a broad wooden balcony, which was always well furnished with flowers summer and winter. At this season there were boxes of mignonette among the autumn flowers, and the perfume floated into the room on the cool night air.

Sir Allan left the pistol case open upon the centre table, amongst a litter of magazines and newspapers. He had been too well waited on all his life ever to have acquired the habit of putting things away. He left everything to be cared for by that inferior race, whose duty it is to follow in the footsteps of a grand seigneur, and to protect his property from the consequences of his own carelessness.

When her husband was gone, Clare Darnel looked up at the clock on the mantelpiece. It was five minutes past eleven. She could hear doors being shut upon the ground floor; all the sounds of a household retiring for the night.

"I can take an hour before midnight," she said to herself, as she began her letter to the friend of her childhood, that one trusted friend from whom she had no secrets.

She had not been writing ten minutes when the window which she left ajar was slowly pushed open, and a man stepped noiselessly into the room. She heard no footfall on the velvet pile, but went on writing, calm, beautiful in the lamplight, an image of domestic peace, the fire-light shining on the dark folds of her satin gown. For some moments she wrote on, while the man stood watching her, holding his breath. Then she heard his breathing, short and quick, like a dog's. She looked up in sudden fear, and saw a tall, wasted figure in a worn-out velveteen coat, a haggard face looking down at her.

It was her husband's face as she had seen it many a time after dissipated habits had ruined his health. It was her son's face, aged by seven years' apprenticeship to the devil since she had last looked upon those features. It was the face of the man whom Colonel Stukely and Grace had seen on the common.

"Valentine," she ejaculated in a half whisper, wringing her hands. "How can you come here —like a thief in the night?"

"How else can I come? It is the only fashion in which I am allowed to enter my mother's house."

"It is not my house. It is Sir Allan's house; and you have no right to enter it without his permission. Oh, my God, what has come to you? How have you fallen into this despicable state—after the sums of money that I have sent you?"

"Tens and twenties dribbled out at odd times and seasons," answered her son sulkily. "Money given in that fashion never does a man much good. I wanted capital to start in a new line. I had all manner of golden opportunities, if you would have helped me, as I wanted you to help me, at the right moment. But it was always the same story. You feared to trust me with a large sum of money. You, Lady Darnel, mistress of this house, talked of five hundred pounds as if it were half a million. You knew my disposition too well. The usual preachment. You would send me twenty pounds a month, and I must contrive to live respectably upon it. Do you think in this go-a-head age a man can get a fair start in life upon a capital of five pounds."

"I have sent you fifties and hundreds for your debts."

"Yes, when I was on the brink of dangers that would have brought disgrace upon you and your swell husband."

"Valentine, how have you come to such a pass?" asked his mother, waving aside his reproaches, which were not new to her. "You look like a beggar."

"I look like what I am," he answered sullenly. "I have had a run of bad luck—cards, horses—everything has gone wrong with me. Other men—cads, with half my brains—can make fortunes. I, with three times their education, only risk my wretched pittance to lose it. Do you think a man of my temper could be content to live upon five pounds a week, while there was a gaming-table or a race-course in the world on which he could try to quadruple it?"

"A gambler, Valentine! Another of your father's vices."

"What else do I inherit from him? Not money, or position. And your d—— cleverness deprived me of even his name. I am always being asked to what Stuarts I belong? What account can I give of myself, do you think? I would rather have been free to answer, 'I am Valentine Mackenzie, the son of the man who drank himself mad, and shot the sentry at Mallow.'"

"You are cruel to the last degree—cruel to reduce yourself to this degraded position—cruel to creep into this house—cruel to me now as you were cruel when you were a boy—as your father was before you," said Clare Darnel, beside herself with the agony of her fears, "you have no right in this house, where there are only good people, people who fear God and respect themselves. You do neither. I say you have no right here."

"And I tell you that wherever my mother is I have a right to be. I suppose you have kept my existence a secret. Your swell husband does not even know there is such a person: but by heaven he shall know!"

He spoke in a hoarse, muffled voice, which

grew louder with his indignation against fate and his mother. At any moment that sound of voices might awaken Sir Allan in the next room. Clare hurried to the door of communication. It was shut. She drew across a velvet curtain which draped the door, and which would help to muffle the sound of those agitated voices.

"He knows that I had a son," she said, "but when I married him I believed that you were dead, that you had been lost in the Erl King. Although all the happiness of my life depended upon that marriage, I would not have married him if I had known that you were living. No, by heaven, I loved him too well to bring such a curse upon him as a stepson with your vices."

"Well, he has me and my vices; and he and you had better make the best of me. What are you going to do for me, MOTHER?" the tender name was uttered with a cynical laugh.

"What *can* I do. If I give you money you will throw it away on a race-course or at a gambling-table: whatever I do for you it all comes to the same thing. You will drink, squander and degrade yourself to the condition in which you come to me to night, the condition of a beggar."

"Because you never give me enough money. Give me a round sum—three or four hundred pounds for instance—that would start me in a new country."

"How often have you talked of starting afresh, promised to begin a new life?" questioned his mother bitterly. "I gave you a hundred pounds to furnish an apartment in Paris. You were to study art, you were to live as other students live there—cheaply, unpretentiously, till you could earn your own maintenance. For a few months things seemed to be going well with you. I hoped you were living comfortably on the twenty pounds a month which I sent you. Then came a long story of difficulties, debts of honour, a mysterious entanglement which might lead to exposure in the newspapers; and I had to send another hundred pounds. You have drained me of the income my generous husband settled on me, and which I told him was three times too much for my wants. I have been sneered at, talked about, for spending so little money, for dressing worse than other women in my position."

"You look an object of compassion at this moment," said her son, surveying her with a diabolical sneer.

Her plainly-made black satin dinner gown, becoming in its severe simplicity, seemed to him the height of luxury. It was not for him to know that the gown had been worn two winters. Men of his stamp always think a woman is well enough dressed so long as her gown holds together. The wives of such men are supposed to have no right to complain while their clothes are wind and weather proof.

Lady Darnel took her porte-monnaie from her pocket.

"Here are six sovereigns and some silver, Valentine," she said, offering him the contents; "all I have in the world, or am likely to have, until Christmas."

He took the money carelessly, indifferently.

"It will be very little good," he said, "beyond getting me a week's lodging, and a slop suit in which I shall look a little worse than in these rags. I tell you that what I want—the only thing that can do me any good—is a round sum of money. I know of a splendid opening. A friend of mine owns a vineyard near Cadiz. It only wants working to produce as fine a sherry as the best that is made in the district. And he would take me into partnership, if I could give him three or four hundred on the nail, and could pledge myself to produce as much more a year hence. That would mean not a beggarly pittance, but a trade, a fortune. You would not be ashamed to own a wholesale dealer in Spanish wines for your son. The trade is reputable, even if the wines are doctored. Come, mother, don't tell me you can't find this money. You have but to ask Sir Allan."

"I will not ask him. No, Valentine, even if I believed in the possibility of your redemption, I would not ask that generous man to give me more money, when of his own accord he has given me three times too much for all my reasonable requirements. But I have no hope of your reform. I know that if I gave you three hundred pounds to-night it would go just as the other money has gone. The utmost I will do for you, the uttermost that duty constrains me to do, is to provide you with the means of living decently from week to week. That I will do, and no more. And even to do that I shall have to borrow money. Your demands have completely exhausted my resources."

"Very good. Then I must have recourse to someone else. There is a lady in this house upon whom my claim is second only to my claim upon you."

"A lady in this house?" repeated Clare, aghast with wonder.

"Grace Darnel is my affianced wife. I believe a man has some kind of claim upon the woman who has promised to marry him."

"My step-daughter, Grace, affianced to you,

to you, Valentine Mackenzie! You must be mad to say such a thing!"

"The statement may sound preposterous, but it is true. Miss Darnel took it into her head to work at the Louvre just at the time I was working there. You think very likely that I never did so work, that my art education was altogether a sham. But there you belie me. I worked honestly enough till I got sick of an impossible profession. No matter, I was attracted by the young lady's appearance, was able to pay her some small attention, and saw that she was pleased with me. I contrived to question her duenna. I heard that she was Miss Darnel, of Darnel Park, an heiress. The imbroglio became interesting; and I determined to try my chances with Miss Darnel, whom I really admired more than any girl I had seen for an age."

"What an honour for Grace!"

"I contrived to get upon confidential terms with her, and soon found the key to her heart. She is a generous, high-spirited girl, full of romance. Just the girl to think the world well lost for love. We were desperately in love with each other. A sharp attack of—of—an old complaint of mine brought me to death's door."

"Was it your father's malady, the dire disease that comes from intemperance, Valentine?" asked his mother, looking at him intently, seeing only too plainly in his haggard face the same indications which she had seen so often in the face of her dead husband.

"No matter what it was. I wrote to Miss Darnel from my sick bed. She answered as a true-hearted girl might be expected to answer. She promised to be my wife. I have that promise under her own hand. She will be of age in a year. And as soon as she is of age and her own mistress I shall claim the fulfilment of that promise."

"Does she know who you are?"

"Well, not exactly. When you are in Rome do as the Romans do, says the proverb. When I was in Paris I was a Frenchman. One alias is as good as another. In Paris I was not Valentine Stuart, but Victor de Camillac."

"And you come to this house—an adventurer, an impostor, a swindler—to claim the promise made by a credulous girl, your dupe and victim. You, my son, would do this thing? This is the deepest disgrace you have threatened me with yet!"

"It is for you to work out the problem so as to avoid disgrace. Give me three or four hundred pounds and I will start for Cadiz to-morrow, to return a year hence as a respectable merchant, and to claim my betrothed. She will pardon my change of name and nationality; if I can stand before her as a gentleman, and your son. She is so fond of you that the relationship will be an additional claim to her regard."

"Do not think that I will ever sanction any engagement between you and Grace. Not if you could struggle out of the abyss into which your degrading habits have sunk you—not even if you could come here in outward seeming a gentleman. Never would I sanction the union of that good and true-hearted girl with your father's son. The cup of despair which I drained to the dregs shall never be offered to her, while I have power to prevent that infamy. Sir Allan knows what you were as a boy. If the worst come to the worst he shall know what you are as a man."

"Wouldn't it be wiser for your own sake if you were to temporize—let me go to Spain, work out my own redemption, and return worthy of Grace—and of you. I will do it, mother, if you will trust me."

He laid his hand upon his mother's shoulder; he looked at her pleadingly as she stood with clasped hands, an image of despair. It was the first time that he had touched her since they entered; he, the son whom she had not seen for seven years.

"I cannot trust you," she answered, not in unkindness but in despair. "I have been too often deceived. I know your nature too well. I will do what I can for you, but it must be in my own way. Oh, Valentine, why do you follow in the fatal road that your father trod to his doom? The habits of the drunkard and the gambler ruined him; and they will ruin you if you do not reform. Think of his dreadful end—a murderer, a lunatic. Be warned in time. No, my poor son, it is not yet too late. I will help you. I will visit you, befriend you in every way, if you will only show a real purpose of amendment. And now, for pity's sake, leave this house, before Sir Allan overhears anything. Are you lodging in the village?"

"I have been lodging under hedges and haystacks since yesterday evening. When I landed at Newhaven yesterday morning I had just enough to pay for a third-class ticket to London, and another third-class ticket to Scadleigh. I have been roaming about ever since, with empty pockets and an empty stomach, watching for a chance of an interview with you or Grace."

"Thank God, you did not see Grace—in this dreadful plight. Poor creature—poor unhappy boy," said Lady Darnel, glancing at the clock. "Ten minutes to twelve; they will hardly have gone to bed at the Coach and Horses, for they seldom close until after eleven. You had better go there, and get a room for the night. There is a sheltered lane at the back of the inn garden—a narrow lane with tall hedges. I will meet you there at seven to-morrow morning, and we can talk quietly, we can make some plan for your future. And now, go. There is not a moment to be lost, if you want to get shelter to-night."

"I don't want to sleep under a hedge," he said sullenly, moving slowly towards the window, reluctant, undecided.

At this moment the door leading into the corridor was opened a little way, and a sweet girlish voice said, "Mother, are you still up?"

Lady Darnel rushed to the door, and met Grace before she could enter the room.

"Yes, dear child," she said, going out into the corridor, and shutting the door behind her. "Oh, Grace, why are you not in bed? It is close upon midnight, and you were up at four."

"I couldn't sleep a wink, if I went to bed. Mayn't I come into your room for a few minutes' chat?"

"Not to-night. It is too late."

"How pale you are, mother! Are you ill?"

"No, no, not ill, only a little tired. I have

sat up too long. Now, Grace, I shall take you back to your room, and you must go to bed instantly."

The girl was in her dressing gown, her splendid brown hair hanging loose upon her shoulders. Lady Darnel put her arm round her and led her along the corridor. Grace's rooms were opposite those inhabited by Sir Allan and Lady Darnel. These three had exclusive occupation of this southern wing. The central portion of the first floor was taken up by a picture gallery and a billiard room. Miss Darnel's rooms were in the northern wing.

"What has made you so wakeful, Gracie?" asked Clare, when she had taken the girl back to her room.

Grace hesitated for a few moments, looking at the ground, and playing nervously with the lace upon her dressing gown.

She was longing to tell all her troubles to her stepmother, yet dared not. Fear of her father's anger kept her dumb.

"Oh, I don't know," she said. "Perhaps it was the exciting idea of our Italian tour. At any rate, I couldn't sleep; and I thought if you were up I should like to have a talk. But you are too tired and you ought to go to bed. You are as white as a ghost."

"Yes, I am very tired. Good night, dear child."

"Good night, mother," and with an affectionate kiss they parted.

Lady Darnel did not go back to her room immediately. She wanted time—first to be sure that Grace did not follow her; secondly, to recover her coolness of brain, to consider quietly and calmly if possible, what was to be done with this foolish son of hers. He would have gone when she went back to her room perhaps; or if he had not gone she would be better able to reason with him after a few minutes' quiet.

She walked up and down the corridor two or three times, thinking deeply, trying to hit upon some line of conduct which might save Grace and reclaim the prodigal. Grace must on no account know that her lover was in the neighbourhood. Girls are so foolish. His wretched condition would appeal to her pity. There is no knowing into what foolishness she might be entrapped.

The stable clock, and the church clock, struck twelve—the last with silvery solemn tone heard from afar across the elms and oaks, the dells and slopes where the cattle were lying at rest. Lady Darnel took one turn more.

"Hark! What can that be?"

No doubt as to what it was. The report of a pistol. What it meant was another thing.

For a moment or so Clare Darnel stood motionless with terror. Then there came the thud of a heavy fall.

"It is in my room," cried Clare, beside herself with apprehension, remembering the revolvers in their case on the table, the open case with dark red velvet lining glowing in the lamp-light. She had looked at it absently while Valentine was talking to her—looked at it with mind so abstracted as never to consider how fatal a thing a revolver may be.

"He has killed himself!" she cried distractedly.

She rushed to her room, tearing at the door with convulsive hands, which made the mere turning of the handle seem a work of time and difficulty. She expected to see her reprobate son stretched upon the floor and weltering in his blood. She knew not that a worse evil had befallen her.

She went into the room. The casement was wide open, and the night wind was blowing in, scattering the papers on her writing table. The doorway leading into the bedroom was open, the velvet *portière* pulled aside, and Allan Darnel was lying across the threshold, bleeding, dead, as his wife thought, in the supreme agony of that moment.

While she stood looking at him, with clasped hands, his daughter rushed into the room, and saw what had happened.

CHAPTER V.

"AS FROM A DREAM OF MURDER."

GRACE'S shrieks rang through the silent house. The wife flung herself on the ground by her husband's side, voiceless, in a dumb agony, clinging to the prostrate form, kissing the pallid face, imploring for a word, a look.

He was loosely dressed in trousers and velvet dressing-gown, dressed like a man who had risen hastily at a strange sound, prepared to face a midnight intruder. His wife opened his dressing-gown, and laid her ear against his breast. Yes, the heart was beating still, feebly as it seemed to her, a beat which might dwindle into silence at any moment, a thread of life that might snap while she listened.

Servants came, sleepy, confused, all talking at once. Then Dora Darnel, very delicate and dainty, in a flowing white garment, with pale pink ribbons; then the Colonel, in an old red velvet dressing-gown, which made him look like a wizard.

"For God's sake, let somebody go for the

doctor," said Clare, without lifting her head; then as Stukely knelt on the other side of his friend's prostrate form, "Oh, Colonel, you can help us. You will know. Is it a dangerous wound? Does it mean death?"

"Not death, no, no. God forbid," said the Colonel. "It is a nasty wound; terrible loss of blood. The bullet has hit rather low, just below the ribs. What was he doing with that accursed revolver?"

"I don't know. They were on the table. He was looking at them an hour ago before he went to bed."

"You don't know," said the Colonel, wonderingly. "Weren't you in the room when it happened?"

"No, I was in the corridor. I had been in Grace's room."

"He was alone then?"

"I—I suppose so."

"Oh, my poor, poor brother," ejaculated Dora. "To think that he should have lifted his hand to take away his own life. He, so good a Christian; he, who used to be so happy."

"How dare you say that he tried to take his his own life," said Clare, not loudly, but with intense indignation. "You know that he is happy. That he has never known a care since he has been my husband; except his too thoughtful care for me. Oh, my darling, what evil things will not be said of me while your voice is silent to defend?" she added, apostrophising her unconscious husband with passionate love.

"There will always be a voice to defend you—were defence needed—while Allan's friend is at your side," said the Colonel quietly.

Purdew, the old butler, was in the room, kneeling by his master. He, too, had seen gun-shot wounds, and he knew that this was a desperate one. With his help Colonel Stukely could have carried his old friend into the next room and laid him on his bed, but after a murmured consultation they agreed that it was wise not to lift him until the surgeon came. The loss of blood might be intensified by any alteration of position. Lady Darnel brought a pillow for her husband's head. A servant brought some brandy, and the Colonel wetted Sir Allan's lips with a little, while Lady Darnel damped his forehead with eau-de-cologne. But there were no signs of returning consciousness.

A groom had ridden off for the doctor. They heard the clatter of hoofs just now galloping along the avenue; but let him gallop as he might, it must be more than half an hour before the doctor could arrive. The Colonel and Purdew did all that could be done to staunch the blood which oozed slowly from Sir Allan's side. It was a terrible half-hour, a half-hour of agony, in which every moment might bring the fatal end of their fainting hopes.

Clare Darnel crouched upon the ground beside her husband, hanging over him, with white lips and despairing eyes, watching his ghastly face with a countenance that was almost as death-like.

"He will die," she kept saying to herself; "he will die by the hand of my son. Oh, God! why did I ever link my accursed life with his?"

Her mind went back to that other night of murder, the report of the gun ringing sharp in the silence of night, startling her from the heavy slumber of sheer exhaustion—the moment of bewilderment and doubt, then the rush to the window to see what had happened. The picture of that vanished scene flashed back upon her as she hung over her husband. The moonlit barrack-yard—doors opening, lights appearing, dark figures crossing the quadrangle, and then a figure carried across the yard by four men. Her first thought had been that it was her husband's figure she saw thus carried—that he had escaped from his room and killed himself. She was to know too soon that the calamity was even worse than this. And now came a second tragedy, a dire and horrible deed which was perhaps to desolate her life for ever. At last there came the sound of horses' hoofs again galloping up the avenue—two horses this time, and sounding in the night silence like six—then the opening of doors below, and then footsteps in the corridor, and the doctor was amidst them, a stout, elderly man, commonplace, but clever, a man to be relied on in calamity.

He put them all aside and knelt down on one knee to examine his patient; and then, without expressing any opinion, he ordered everyone out of the room except the Colonel and Purdew.

"Grace, take care of Lady Darnel," said the Colonel, and Grace put her arm round her step-mother and tried to lead her from the room, the girl blinded by her tears, the woman's eyes dry and burning. She had not yet shed a tear.

"No, Grace," she said, "I will not go away. If I must not stay in this room I will wait in the corridor. I will not go far from Allan."

At the mere mention of her husband's name she burst into a flood of tears, the first relief that had come to her since that first shock of her reprobate son's entrance.

It was in vain that Grace pleaded, in vain that Dora lectured. Clare Darnel would not move beyond the outside of the morning-room door. She knelt with her ear against the keyhole, knelt there, listening, and praying dumbly now and then, till the doctor came out, after a delay of an hour or more.

"Will he die?" she asked, seizing the doctor's arm.

Mr. Danvers, the family doctor, looked grave and shook his head.

"It is a bad case, Lady Darnel."

"But not hopeless—oh, for God's sake say it is not hopeless!"

"We shall have Mr. Friedricson here to-morrow morning," answered the doctor. "He can tell you better than I."

"And my beloved one may die in the night, before help comes. Let me go to him—let me be with him."

"No, Lady Darnel, that is impossible. He must be kept very quiet—there must be no one in the room except Purdew and me. I shall stay here all night."

"Thank God for that! But it is cruel to keep me away from him. Do you think I am a child, that I have no self-command?"

"I think you are a woman, and that you love your husband. No, Lady Darnel, you must not enter that room till Sir Allan is in a less precarious state. You must obey me in this matter—for his sake. I am going to send one of your men with a message to my wife, and then I shall go back to Sir Allan. We shall have a couple of surgical nurses down to-morrow morning."

Clare Darnel wrung her hands in a silent despair. She turned from the doctor and walked quickly to the end of the corridor. Like King David she turned her face to the wall. She felt that there was no comfort—no relief. Her husband was taken away from her—given over to nurses and surgeons, and she was told that she must not enter his room. Her sacred right as his wife was set at nought. Death itself could not have robbed her more utterly of his presence. To sit beside his bed, to watch the changes in his face, to listen to every breath. There would have been comfort in this. But she was to have no comfort. She stood leaning against the moulding of the window-frame at the end of the corridor with her face to the wall.

"My son, my son," she repeated to herself. "I ought never to have married that good man. I was selfish, wicked, blind, to link my miserable lot with his. I am the cause of his death."

Grace came from her room, where she had been sitting with her aunt, who had established herself there uninvited, "to be nearer poor Allan," she said.

"Dear mother, come to my room, come and lie down on my bed," pleaded Grace, and the word mother sounded sweet in Clare Darnel's ears, even in the midst of her despair. The girl's tenderness recalled that revelation of Valentine's.

"No, my darling, *your* life shall not be blighted," she sobbed, drawing Grace to her breast. "You shall not be sacrificed to worthlessness and profligacy."

The strange speech startled Grace. What could it mean? could Lady Darnel know—or suspect anything about her luckless lover—the man she had seen on the common that morning.

She succeeded in getting Lady Darnel to her room, where Dora was sitting piously before an open Testament reading the history of St. Paul's shipwreck, and how the viper came out of the fire and hung upon his arm. It could hardly be particularly comforting in such a moment; but Dora fled to her Bible in calamity as a duty. She did not even wait for calmness and order around her, but sat down in the midst of chaos and read the first chapter that came to hand, in a thoroughly business-like way. By this means she had acquired a stupendous battery of texts, with which she was always ready to open fire in argument or warning.

In Dora's mind even the viper that came out of the fire was not altogether inapplicable to the present state of affairs.

"My poor brother has had a viper hanging upon him," she said to herself. "I knew that misery would come out of that marriage; but I did not think that it would take the form of bloodshed."

Lady Darnel consented to lie down on a sofa wheeled near the fire, to please Grace rather than from any hope of relief to be obtained from repose. A rug was spread over her, and she lay silent, with closed eyes. The other two women might suppose she was sleeping.

"Had you not better go to your own room, Aunt Dora?" said Grace, a little worried by the sight of that calm white-robed figure, and the open Bible. Grace was firm in religious faith and reverence for the Scriptures; but she could not seat herself down to read the Acts of the Apostles with folded hands, in the midst of a domestic convulsion.

"It is nearly two o'clock, Aunt Dora. Do go to your own room," she said, hardly concealing her irritation.

"No, Grace, I like to be near Allan. My own room is at the other end of the house. I hope I am not in your way here."

"Not at all," said Grace shortly; and then she got up and went out to the corridor and listened at her father's door.

Not a sound. But he might die, and she would hear no more than she heard now. It was all so sad, so inexplicable. Her father at death's door: he who had kissed her and bade her good-night in his cheeriest voice only a few hours ago. How had it happened? She had hardly been calm enough even to wonder about it until now; but now she began to ask herself how this tragedy had come to pass.

Could it be the result of accident? Her father, an old cavalry soldier, the hero of two Indian campaigns; was such a man likely to be playing with firearms as children and Cockneys play with such things? Was he likely to handle a revolver so ignorantly or so awkwardly as to lodge its contents in his side? And again she had understood that Sir Allan had gone to bed, and that Lady Darnel was writing alone in her room when she, Grace, knocked at the door.

She longed to see her dear old Colonel. He perhaps might have told her something; yet what could he know more than she, since he had only appeared on the scene after the catastrophe?

She walked up and down the corridor for half an hour or more, till the cold drove her back to her room. It was very cold in that dead hour of the night, and poor Grace was shivering in her muslin dressing-gown when she went back to her room.

Dora Darnel was sitting by the fire, just as Grace had left her, steadily ploughing through the Acts, as if she had been a divinity student preparing for an examination. Lady Darnel lay, with her face hidden, motionless, silent.

"Is she asleep?" enquired Grace, in a low voice.

"I believe so."

Grace threw herself on her bed, and cried herself to sleep, a troubled sleep, easily broken. She had slept thus, hardly for one moment losing the consciousness of her grief, when she was awakened by an agonising cry.

She started up from her pillow to see Dora Darnel standing beside the sofa in the dying firelight looking down at her brother's wife.

Clare was lying on her back, with her clasped hands above her head, her eyes wide open, and the eye-balls fixed in an awful stare.

"My fault, my fault," she cried. "I murdered him."

The aunt and niece looked at each other, appalled, horror-stricken. These words were the words of a dreamer, and dreams are wildest fictions; but such words at such a moment had a thrilling effect.

CHAPTER VI.

"ALL WAS SILENT, ALL WAS GLOOM."

FRIEDRIC FRIEDRICSON, the great surgeon, had come and had gone, and was to come again. So far he had been able to say few words of comfort or of hope. Sir Allan's condition was so precarious that the surgeon had not dared to attempt the extraction of the bullet; and until that was extracted there could be little hope of recovery. The symptomatic fever was more violent than is usual in such cases. The patient was delirious sleepless, and unable to take nourishment. Altogether the case looked threatening.

Lady Darnel's slumbers had not lasted long after that awful dream of hers. At four o'clock in the morning she had awakened, and had gone to Grace's dressing-room to give herself a cold bath, and to dress for the day. And now it was late in the afternoon, and she had not closed her eyes since that troubled sleep on the sofa.

The three women wandered about the house like three ghosts, so pale and wan and silent were they all. Grace turned to Colonel Stukely for her only comfort, Dora read her Bible at all times and seasons. Lady Darnel sought comfort from no one. She paced with noiseless footfall up and down the corridor outside her husband's room for hours at a stretch. She interrogated everybody who came out—the neatly-clad nurse in her prim cap and spotless apron, Danvers, the medical man, Purdew, the old military servant. These were her only sources of comfort; and such comfort as they could give was mixed with gall.

It was some relief to hear of her beloved, to know that he still lived. It was agony to know that the fever raged fiercely, that the delirium continued without abatement. He could recognise no one. What mattered who watched beside his bed, what hireling hands ministered to him?

"He would know me," said Clare piteously, "but they will not let me go to him."

"My dear soul," replied the Colonel soothingly, "he does not even know me, his old comrade of many a forced march. Why he and I have ridden side by side over an Indian desert when we were nodding asleep in our saddles for sheer weariness. We were chums and companions for a quarter of a century, from Eton to the Punjaub: and yet he does not recognise me."

"He would know his wife," said Clare, with conviction.

As the day wore on she could hardly be induced to leave the corridor. Lunch, dinner, all conventional meals were scorned by those three women: but it was only Lady Darnel who had not broken her fast by so much as a biscuit since the previous evening. But at last Grace beguiled her stepmother into her den, and made her sit by the fire and take some tea and bread and butter.

"Do you want to be ill, too, and make us still more unhappy," said Grace reproachfully.

She had insisted on giving Lady Darnel her own bedroom, the door of which was opposite the sick room; while she herself was to occupy a little bed hastily put up in the dressing-room. This arrangement was deeply resented by Dora.

"I think if anybody has a right to be near Allan at such time, it is I, his sister," she said, when she and Grace were alone.

"But surely, Aunt Dora, a wife's right is above all others."

"That depends upon the wife."

"Then, if there can be any such distinction nobody can dispute my stepmother's claim, for she is the most devoted of wives."

"She has a knack of seeming very devoted," remarked Dora.

"Seeming, and a knack!" repeated Grace indignantly. "How can you say such things, Aunt Dora? How dare you insinuate that my father's wife is not true?"

"I insinuate nothing, Grace; and I am not

going to be taken to task by a schoolgirl. I can only say that Lady Darnel is a mystery to me, just as she is a mystery to the county. Indeed I may say that *you* are the only person who appears to understand her and believe in her."

"My father believes in her," retorted Grace, more and more indignant. "That is enough for me."

"Your father is under the spell of a potent fascination, my dear. Have you never heard of a middle-aged widower subjugated by the manœuvres of a handsome widow—a widow whose antecedents are wrapped in profound darkness."

"You are talking most unjustly, Aunt Dora; and what is more you know that you are unjust I wonder you don't expect something to crawl out of your Bible and sting you. I wouldn't sit with my Bible on my lap and spit venom at innocent people."

"If you cannot control your tongue, Grace, I shall go to my own room," said Dora, closing her Bible, and rising as if to depart.

"I shall be very much beholden to my tongue if it drives you there," retorted Grace, upon which Miss Darnel had no option, and was obliged to carry out her threat; more especially as the room was Grace's own particular den, and she was only a visitor there.

She departed, carrying her Bible and a large assortment of angry feelings with her.

But she did not retire to the solitude of her own apartments in the north wing. Solitude is apt to be intolerable in these periods of suspense and anxiety. Miss Darnel went down to the drawing-room, and on her way met a servant who was going upstairs to announce Mr. Colchester.

He was in the drawing-room, the man said, and wanted to see Lady Darnel, Miss Grace, anybody.

Dora felt that she came under the last head; so she hurried to the drawing-room, eager to be *en rapport* with the county; though, indeed, in spite of his splendid position, she always looked upon Edward Colchester as in somewise an outsider. He was so good-natured, so hail-fellow-well-met with all the world, so little governed by the Draconian laws of society.

She found him in the drawing-room, in hunting clothes, fidgetting about with a crop in his hand, just as if he had that moment dismounted to rest his hunter's back during a pause in the morning's work.

"My dear Miss Darnel," he cried, seizing her hand, "what a dreadful thing this is? Been out with Colonel Thorpe's harriers; only just heard it on my way home, or should have been here before. How did it happen? Is he very bad? How is Grace?"

He forgot himself in his agitation, and said Grace *tout court.*

"It is a long story, Mr. Colchester; and it is a profound mystery. We none of us know what it all means yet. My poor brother is in a most precarious state. I fear we may lose him."

Here the tears rushed to her eyes; and they were not crocodile tears. If she hated her brother's wife, she loved her brother; and though she could not bear to see him happy in his second marriage, nay, resented that second marriage as if it were a deadly wrong done to herself, she could not calmly contemplate the possibility of losing him.

"Don't cry," said Colchester, very much inclined to be tearful himself. "Things are never so bad as they look. Doctors are such regular old ravens, don't you know. They like to frighten us out of our wits, in order to take credit for their wonderful cleverness when the patient pulls through. We pulled him through they say, and then we poor fools pay their big bills without blinking. But for goodness sake tell me how it happened? Sir Allan shot himself they say; late last night, after you had all gone to bed."

"Not *all*," said Dora. "Lady Darnel sat up late to write letters. She was still up at the time it happened."

"Then she must know all about it."

"She appears to know nothing. She had been to Grace's room. She was in the corridor when she heard the pistol go off."

"And Sir Allan was alone in his room?"

"So it appears. He had gone to bed an hour before. He must have got up and gone back to Lady Darnel's morning-room, where he had left the case of revolvers on the table. Why he should have got up and half-dressed himself, and gone back to get those pistols, is an unfathomable mystery."

"He may have heard burglars—or fancied he heard them," suggested Colchester. "Some men are always on the *qui vive* for burglars—sleep with life-preservers under their pillows. They might burgle all round my house and I should never hear 'em; but I know it is a weakness with some men. How do you know that there wasn't a burglar there? He may have shot Sir Allan."

Dora shook her head.

"I do not believe it was a burglar. If there had been any one in the house—any scuffle between Sir Allan and a robber—Lady Darnel must have heard it. She was in the corridor when the pistol went off."

"Then how do you solve the mystery?"

"It is my painful conviction that the deed was either murder or suicide."

"Suicide," exclaimed Colchester. "Out of the question. Why, there wasn't a happier fellow in Wilts than Sir Allan; the cheeriest, the kindest, the most genial of men."

"Kind, genial, I admit," said Dora, "but I know my brother better than anyone else can know him. I was his companion and confidante from the time I left school till the day he married his second wife. I do not believe that he has been happy of late. His marriage was not a satisfactory marriage. Even if he himself could have felt thoroughly satisfied—which I do not think he ever did—he knew that the county was dissatisfied with his choice. He knew that the cloud of mystery which surrounded Lady Darnel's antecedents cast a dark shadow upon an old and honoured family. People might like and esteem him; but they could not esteem a woman of whom they were told nothing, who was foisted upon them without a word of explanation. And so they naturally fell away from their old friend; and, although my brother pretended to take the matter lightly, I believe that he was cut to the quick."

"The county are a —— set of snobs," said young Colchester, swallowing an evil word with a wry face. "Why couldn't they take such a splendid woman as Lady Darnel on trust?"

"My dear Mr. Colchester, I am thankful to know that in good society no one is ever taken on trust," replied Miss Darnel. "What would society be like if people were?"

"Perhaps a good deal pleasanter than it is now," retorted the reprobate squire, who troubled himself much less about the antecedents of an acquaintance than about the pedigree of a fox-hound.

"No, Mr. Colchester," continued Dora Darnel, "my poor brother has not been happy of late. There are mysterious circumstances connected with his marriage that I have not been able to fathom; but I am not a fool, and in spite of all outward appearances I have seen enough to know that Allan is not happy. This sudden idea of going off to winter in Italy is so unlike him—such a complete breaking up of the life he loves—that the notion could only have arisen out of a disturbed state of mind."

"But, my dear Miss Darnel, the physician ordered——" interrupted Colchester.

"Physicians may be inspired to order anything. They are often only the mouthpieces of their patients. If this dreadful event is not the work of my brother's own hand, in an interval of despair, why then we have to look for a still darker solution of the mystery, and to ask where is the murderer?"

"I say burglar," protested Colchester. "Sir Allan heard a man in the room next his own, got up, put on his coat, challenged the man. Burglar saw revolvers on table, snatched up one and shot Sir Allan—or shot him with a revolver of his own, just as likely."

"Would a burglar enter a room in which there were two lamps burning—a room evidently occupied?"

"Burglars have cheek enough for anything. No doubt Lady Darnel keeps her jewels in her bedroom, women always do."

Miss Darnel shrugged her shoulders, with the air of declining to waste any more time in argument with a person of Mr. Colchester's limited intellect.

"I should very much like to see Grace," he said, getting very red, and faltering a little, "if she is not too bad to see anyone."

"She may not be too bad to see you," replied Dora. "I dare say her taste for hunting will survive the calamity that has fallen upon us."

"True," answered Colchester simply. "She may

like to know where next week's meets are to be, even though she can't go out. She is always interested in the hounds. Perhaps she would like to have a couple of puppies at walk. They might be an amusement to her while there is illness in the house. But I trust in God poor Sir Allan will pull through quicker than you expect."

Dora rang the bell, and sent a servant for her niece. Mr. Colchester walked up and down the room meanwhile, sorely troubled, and finding no word to say to his companion.

The footman came back to say that Miss Grace Darnel sent her compliments to Mr. Colchester, and was much too unhappy to see anyone.

"Thank'ee," said the young squire; and when the man was gone he added moodily, "I didn't much think she'd see me. She's been uncommonly rough on me for the last year or so. And before she went to school in Paris we were no end of chums. Good-bye, Miss Darnel; I shall call again to-morrow, and perhaps Lady Darnel will be well enough to see me. I have always been one of her warmest admirers, you know, and I—well, it would take a dooced lot of hard facts to make me believe that her influence upon Sir Allan's life has been anything but a good influence, and that he isn't as happy as a bird in his marriage with her."

And with these words Mr. Colchester departed, feeling more easy in his mind after he had thus expressed himself.

The vicar's wife and the doctor's old maiden sister called in the course of the afternoon, full of friendliness, and anxious to see Lady Darnel, were she able to receive a friend. The county sent cards and inquiries, but offered no warmer form of sympathy. And so the long day of grief and fear wore on, to be followed by another sleepless night, and a dawn of sorrow. There was no improvement in the patient. The utmost comfort Mr. Danvers could offer was the assurance that he saw no increase of danger.

Dora and Grace went down to the dining-room to breakfast on this second morning; but Lady Darnel could not be induced to leave her room. There she was close to the sick-chamber. There she was within call at any moment should her husband recover his senses, and ask for her. There, too, she was secure from the horror of strange faces, the agony of having to go on with the routine of daily life. She was shut in from the outer world—her own mistress.

Grace had anxieties of her own, as well as that agonizing fear for her father's life. She wanted very much to have a few words with her godfather; and on Miss Darnel retiring to her daily interview with the housekeeper the desired opportunity occurred. Grace and Colonel Stukely were alone.

"Have you seen anything more of him?" she asked, plunging at once into the heart of her subject. "Have you heard anything?"

"Not a word," replied the Colonel. "I took a long walk yesterday afternoon with the idea that I might find out something. I called at the inn, saw the landlord, and asked if he had had any strangers lodging in his house. Not a mortal. Then I went the round of the better class of cottagers, mostly pensioners of yours and Lady Darnel's, to whom you have introduced me at odd times. I didn't put my questions directly, but let out our idea of a burglary at Darnel, and asked if strangers had been noticed about the place. I even walked across to Handlebury Union, with the notion that it was just possible the poor fellow may have had to take refuge there."

"Oh, Colonel, how utterly dreadful."

"My dear child, the Union has sheltered better men than he. However, no such person had been heard of there. So I take it Mr. Camillac must have had a few shillings about him in spite of his wretched appearance, and that he has gone on to some other place. The mystery is that he should have come here at all, unless with the idea of seeing you."

"I feel convinced that he came here to see me, and for no other purpose; and that he is lying dead or dying on some dreary common, where the foxhounds are more likely to find him than anybody else," said Grace impetuously. "Oh, what double misery. Victor dying, or dead—my father's life trembling in the balance. It seems as if the world were coming to an end."

In vain the Colonel argued with his goddaughter, urging that in life the unforeseen is always likely; and that there was no reason to grieve for the fate of a young man who had, perhaps, already fallen on his feet. Grace was not to be comforted. The romantic fancy which had induced her to pledge her young life to this stranger was a folly of the past; but all her womanly feelings were enlisted by her lover in the hour of his helplessness and destitution.

"To think of me, surrounded with all these luxuries," she exclaimed, looking angrily at the richly-furnished breakfast-table, "while the man who was to be my husband has not as good a shelter as the stable dogs."

"My dear child, a young man's life is generally a fact of his own making," said the Colonel sagely. "A man of education, such as you describe this Camillac, could hardly fall so low except through his own misconduct."

"You said that before," retorted Grace. "Pray don't sermonize. If I were not so anxious about my father I would take a couple of dogs and ride over every bit of waste ground within ten miles, till I found that poor fellow."

"If that is your idea, Grace, I can carry it out for you, dogs and all," said the Colonel kindly.

"Oh, my dear godfather, how good you are," cried the girl, repenting of her rudeness. "Forgive me for my ingratitude just now. I hardly know what I say. I am so very miserable—about Victor—about my father and Lady Darnel, most of all."

"Poor Lady Darnel; yes, your father's accident is a terrible blow for her."

"It is not that only," said Grace, dropping her voice, and drawing a little nearer to the Colonel. "But it is all so strange—so full of mystery."

And then she told Colonel Stukely how she had been awakened by a cry of agony from Lady Darnel, and of those strange words spoken in a dream. "My fault, my fault—I murdered him!"

"Was not that strange?" asked Grace, with a troubled look.

"Only strange as dreams are strange. Would

you accuse Lady Darnel of having shot her husband upon such evidence? She fell asleep with her mind full of death and murder, and dreamt that she herself had fired the fatal shot, or had been individually concerned in the deed. Dreams are for the most part sheer lunacy. God knows what hideous visions her troubled brain may have woven."

"Yes, that is just what I thought at the time. But the words have haunted me ever since. You know how fond I am of Lady Darnel. I believe I love her almost as well as I could have loved my own dear mother, had God spared her to me. And yet there are times when I feel worried and perplexed about the mystery of her past life. Aunt Dora says such cruel things."

"My dear, it is in your aunt's nature to say cruel things, just as it is in the nature of wasps and hornets to sting. I don't wish to be rude about your family, but I fancy that old Sir George Darnel's second wife must have introduced a particularly venomous strain into the fine old stock. It is a good thing for the race that Miss Darnel has remained a spinster."

"Yes, Aunt Dora has a peculiar talent for being disagreeable, and she has exercised it unsparingly with regard to Lady Darnel. I always take my stepmother's part; and yet in these last dreadful days Aunt Dora's insinuations about the mystery in her past life have made me miserable. If I were once to believe that she is a hypocrite, that her devotion to my father is only a clever piece of acting——"

"Have no such doubt, no such fear, Grace," said the Colonel heartily. "Your father has told me—his old friend—the whole story of Lady Darnel's life. There is no mystery, nothing that could not be told as freely to you as to me, if your father were so minded. He has held back the knowledge from you only because the story is a dark story. If you knew all you would know that Lady Darnel's first marriage was a time of martyrdom, that as wife and as mother she has been a martyr."

"I did not even know that she had any children," said Grace.

"Yes, there was a son, but he is dead, happily."

"He was a bad son, then?"

"A very bad son—following in the footsteps of a guilty father. Your stepmother's life has been blameless—it has been even heroic. You cannot love her too well."

"And I have loved her with all my heart," answered Grace. "And I will go on loving her. And I will trust her implicitly, come what may.

Dear old godfather, I feel ever so much happier after this talk with you."

"And I'll order my horse and scour the country in search of this ragamuffin suitor of yours," said the Colonel; and to himself he added, "and if I find him it shall go hard if I don't buy him off pretty cheap, and set this little fool of mine free to smile upon honest Ted Colchester."

CHAPTER VII.

"LOVE WILL HAVE HIS DAY."

THE third day began, and still no change in the patient. Mr. Colchester had called on the day before. He called again at breakfast time on this third morning, on his way home after cub-hunting, apologetic about his mud-bespattered boots. The footman ushered him into the dining-room, and he found himself face to face with Grace Darnel before he had time to collect his thoughts.

"So glad to see you again; so sorry to hear Sir Allan is no better," he faltered, as they shook hands. "A capital run; found at Ringtree Marsh, quarter past six; ran him into Milksham Copse, over Chicksand Common, back again into Milksham, got him out into the fields, ran right away to Patsfield over some stiffish country, lost him in Swatley Wood after forty minutes' hard going, started another at half-past seven. But I ought not to talk to you about such things when you are all so unhappy," said Colchester, suddenly aware that he was behaving like a brute, as he saw the blank faces of the two women.

The Colonel looked a little interested, in spite of his anxiety.

"Will you take a cup of tea, or may I give you some coffee?" asked Dora solemnly.

"Thank you. I should like some tea above all things."

The butler had arranged a place for the dropper-in at Grace's right hand, and had put a dish of cutlets in front of that place, by way of invitation; so Mr. Colchester sat down and took his cup of tea. He was much too agitated to eat anything, in spite of his three or four hours in the cold morning air and his forty minutes across country. He thought it an extraordinary privilege to be sitting next Grace, to be able to look at her and talk to her. Yesterday he had been favoured with a second interview with Dora, which had been depressing to the last degree. Grace looked very miserable; but oh, how pretty she was in her misery, and how many years of his life he would have bartered for the power to console her. But he could do nothing except steal a look at her every now and then as he drank his tea.

"When do you begin your regular season?" asked Colonel Stukely, after silence had prevailed for some minutes.

"Not till next month. We shall finish our cub-hunting this week, and then we shall have a few bye days. Our first advertised meet is to be on the fifth of October. I hope all will be well here ever so long before then, and that—if you don't go to Italy—you'll be out and in full force on that day," added Mr. Colchester, looking at Grace.

"I don't suppose I shall ever hunt again," said Grace, bursting into tears; and the Lord of the Manor felt that he was an undisciplined brute, always blurting out foolish speeches, and that there was no help for him.

The butler came back at this moment, with an unusually solemn air, as of one who only carries messages of vital import. He bore a silver salver with a card upon it, which he offered to Miss Darnel.

"The gentleman says that he is here by appointment, ma'am."

"Show him into the library," said Dora, rising with a stately air. "Kindly excuse me, Mr. Colchester."

"I am going this instant, I ought not to have stayed so long," said Colchester apologetically, getting up hurriedly.

But nobody was thinking about him, or how long he stayed. Grace had gone over to her aunt.

"Who is this person, Aunt Dora?" she asked anxiously, "another doctor?"

"No, it is a person on business. A person whom I sent for," answered Miss Darnel. "I don't think I need make any concealment of the matter. The person is a detective from Scotland Yard."

"A detective, Aunt Dora? A detective in this house; summoned by you?"

"Why not, child? If you are indifferent as to the manner in which your father received the wound which may be his death, if you and Lady Darnel, his wife and his daughter, are content to sit down and let the murderer escape, I, his sister, am not so content. The mystery ought to be fathomed: and as there is no one in this house clever enough to fathom it, I have sent for professional assistance."

"You may have acted wisely in so doing," replied Colonel Stukely, "but it would have been more friendly to acquaint Sir Allan's daughter and his old comrade, before you took such a serious step; not to mention his wife, who had a still better claim to be told."

"I'm very glad you've got a detective," said Colchester, "for I believe he'll be of my way of thinking, and scent a burglar in this business. Good-bye. I'll come round again in the afternoon, if I may, just to see how things are going on."

"Come as often as you like, Colchester," replied the Colonel heartily. "Your presence will do something towards cheering us."

Grace shook her head despondingly.

"Nothing can cheer us till my father is out of danger," she said, as Edward Colchester backed out of the room, entangling himself with his spurs, and looking at her adoringly to the last.

"As this kind of thing is altogether out of your line, Miss Darnel, I think it would be as well for me to see the detective with you," said the Colonel, "that is to say, if you wish to see him at all. I could spare you the painful interview altogether, as I can give the man all the information necessary. I am not a stranger to this kind of enquiry."

"I would much rather see the person myself," replied Dora, with an offended air. "I sent for him upon my own responsibility; and I particularly desire that he should know *my* ideas about this terrible event."

"If you take my advice you will tell him no ideas of your own or anyone else's," answered the Colonel sharply. "Give him nothing but the plain facts; and let him work out the solution of the problem in his own way. The detective police are not heaven-born geniuses; but most of them are hard-headed sensible men, and not likely to go far astray, except when they are muddled and misdirected by non-professional interference."

"I do not think you have any reason to consider me either a child or an idiot, Colonel Stukely," retorted Miss Darnel. "Pray permit me to manage my own affairs. You can go with me to the library, if you please."

The Colonel did please, and followed the lady closely, while Grace went upstairs to her step-mother, who sat by the fire, motionless, apathetic. The dainty little breakfast-table beside her was scarcely disturbed from the neat order in which it had been brought into the room.

"You have eaten positively nothing, mother," said Grace, scrutinising the table.

"I have had some tea, and a little toast; I have done very well," answered Clare, and then in a despairing tone she added, "Oh, Grace, there is no improvement. I spoke to one of the nurses. She was going off to her bedroom, with such an orderly air, as if life or death were all the same to her. There is no diminution of the fever—the temperature is just as high. He has not spoken one sensible word since that night. Mr. Friedricson is to come again to-day; but the nurse thinks it would be madness to attempt to extract the bullet while Allan is in this state. I do not believe these people have any hope of saving him."

"Oh, mother, we *must* save him. God will answer our prayers," cried Grace. "Let us pray for that dear life together, side by side, with heart, and strength, and mind. Surely God must hear and answer such prayers?"

In the library Mr. Penwern, a homely-looking, middle-aged man, with pepper-and-salt hair and whiskers, and pepper-and-salt clothing to match, was listening and questioning, and making notes, until he had the story of Sir Allan's wound, so far as it was known to Miss Darnel and Colonel Stukely, all in black and white before him. Then he went up to see the room in which the catastrophe happened, and, moving to and fro, quietly, lest he should disturb the patient in the adjoining room, he made a complete inspection of the ground. Here was the spot, just inside the threshold, where Sir Allan was found lying. There were stains of blood upon the Aubusson carpet to mark the place where he lay while they waited for the coming of the doctor. He had clutched the portière as he fell, for the first three or four hooks that sustained it were wrenched from the brass rod. There was Lady Darnel's writing table. She had been sitting there writing ten minutes before she heard the pistol shot from the corridor outside. There were the two French windows opening on to the balcony.

Was either of these windows open on the night? Yes, one was open. The Colonel remembered the wind blowing in his face as he came in at the door.

Mr. Penwern stepped out upon the balcony and made his survey. It was a broad, old-fashioned balcony, roofing in a colonnade outside the breakfast-room below. The iron pilasters of the colonnade were covered with greenery—a mighty wisteria spread itself along the ironwork like a curtain, an old magnolia was trained over one side of the balcony. Easy enough for any active man to scale such a balcony. No difficulty as to access. The next question to be considered was motive.

"Any valuables kept at this end of the house?" asked the detective.

"Lady Darnel has some jewellery in her dressing-room," answered Dora, "but Lady Darnel's are not family jewels, not of sufficient renown to tempt a thief, I should think."

"Thieves are easily tempted now-a-days," answered Penwern. "The trade is over-run, and business is often slack. It seems to me that this balcony is about the easiest access all along this side of the house, and the point at which any man would naturally enter."

"But with this room occupied; with lamps burning?" suggested Dora incredulously.

"The room had been deserted for some minutes before the shot was fired. A man might have been on the watch for this opportunity."

"Surely he would have waited till Lady Darnel had gone to bed; till the house was dark. That seems only reasonable," said Dora.

"It seems reasonable; but there is the fact that the shot was fired, and there is the antecedent fact that Sir Allan got up and came to that door yonder. I take it that he heard a strange footstep in this room, and that he came in just in time to surprise the burglar. Are you sure that there were no valuables kept in this very room?"

"Quite sure," answered Dora. "It is Lady Darnel's boudoir. There has never been anything kept here except her workboxes and writing-cases, and books, just as you see them now."

The detective had devoured the room with his eyes. He knew every article it contained.

"In that Italian cabinet, for instance, are no

valuables — trinkets, money — kept there?" he asked.

"Nothing of the kind, to my knowledge."

"Stay," exclaimed the Colonel. "Sir Allan told us that he had drawn four hundred pounds in bank-notes for travelling expenses. How do we know that he did not keep the money in this room—in that cabinet, perhaps? I saw him put away a lease in that very cabinet a fortnight ago, when I was here with him and Lady Darnel, at afternoon tea."

"Lady Darnel would be the most likely person to enlighten us, I take it," said the detective, who thirsted to see Lady Darnel.

Until he had scrutinised and taken stock of every member of the family and household it was to Mr. Penwern as if he were playing a difficult game of cards blindfold. When he had seen all his cards he would begin to understand what game he had to play.

After a few minutes' whispered conversation with the Colonel, Dora went in quest of Lady Darnel. She went reluctantly, since she would have preferred that this professional investigation should have been carried on without Lady Darnel's knowledge, a secret underground business, dark as Belzoni's researches in Egyptian tombs. She wanted the thing to be her work, a mystery between her and the detective; to explode at a given moment in a startling revelation which should bring blame and discomfiture on the woman she hated. And now his detested second wife was to be let into the secret, was to have due notice of what was taking place, and would thus be able to prevent discovery were she, as Dora Darnel firmly believed, a guilty agent in the catastrophe.

"If it was her infamy in the past which drove him to suicide, or if it was some lover of hers who stole into the house to murder him, this detective ought to be able to unravel the mystery," Dora told herself, as she went slowly to Grace's bedroom. "But Lady Darnel once on her guard may be able to frustrate him in his investigation, to throw dust in his eyes."

She found Clare Darnel sitting by her neglected fire, just as Grace had left her.

"There is a person here trying to find out the mystery of my brother's wound," she said curtly. "He wants to ask you a few questions."

Clare started suddenly to her feet. That marble face of hers could not grow paler than it had been, but there was a frightened look in her eyes which Dora was quick to perceive.

"What kind of person?" she asked. "A police-officer?"

"He comes from Scotland Yard."

Lady Darnel made no further remark. They went in silence to the morning-room, where Mr. Penwern was standing in front of the window, looking out, while the Colonel fidgetted about by the cold blank hearth.

The detective turned as Lady Darnel entered, saluted her respectfully, and looked at her with grave eyes which absorbed every detail of her appearance, without the faintest indication of eagerness or curiosity.

She stood with her splendid figure drawn to its fullest height, her head erect. Not a vestige of colour varied the marble whiteness of her complexion. The face was colourless and calm as the face of a statue; but the heavy eyelids, the purple shadows round the eyes, told of long agonies of weeping. It was not the first time Clare Darnel had faced the police—had answered to the inquiries in a criminal investigation.

Despite the calm dignity of her attitude, the statuesque repose of her features, the detective saw the signs of apprehension, secret fears which she was struggling to repress.

"This woman knows more than anyone else," he thought, and then he questioned Lady Darnel about the contents of the cabinet.

"Yes," she said dreamily, as if only just remembering the fact, "there are some bank-notes there. The money Sir Allan had drawn for our travelling expenses," her voice faltered a little as she recalled her delight in the idea of that journey, the sweet expectation of happy days with her beloved in a lovely land: and now a grave yawned before her, darkest, direst fears crowded upon her soul.

"A large sum of money?" enquired Penwern.

"Three—no, I think it was four hundred pounds."

"Have you the key of the cabinet, Lady Darnel?"

"My husband and I have duplicate keys—but I doubt if Sir Allan locked the cabinet that night. He had taken out his pistols in order to examine them—he was excited, tired, and did not put the pistols back in the cabinet."

"Will you be good enough to see if the notes are still there, Lady Darnel?" asked the detective.

She started, looked at him curiously, and then a sudden flush crimsoned her cheek and brow.

"What difference can that make?—the notes are safe, of course," she said.

"Not if there was a burglar in this room—and he was clever enough to secure his booty before Sir Allan interrupted him. You don't suppose, Lady Darnel, I take it, that Sir Allan got up out of his bed and came to this room to shoot himself?"

"I. suppose nothing—I know nothing except that my husband's life is in danger."

"The law wants to know a great deal more than that," said Dora. "The law wants to know how my poor brother's life came to be endangered."

"Oblige me by looking for the notes, Lady Darnel," said the detective. "The obvious reading of this sad business is that Sir Allan was shot by a burglar—who managed to escape before you re-entered this room. If so, the burglar must have come after something, and with some definite purpose. Please try the cabinet."

He could see that she was reluctant, curiously reluctant, to obey; but she went slowly to the Italian cabinet and opened the doors to the widest. She had been right in her conjecture—the cabinet had not been locked since Sir Allan took out the pistol-case.

"Do you find the notes, Lady Darnel?" asked Penwern, when she had been standing there some minutes, examining shelves and drawers, and secret—nominally secret—receptacles at the back of the quaint old piece of furniture.

"No, they are not here—at least, I cannot find them."

"Do you know if Sir Allan had taken the numbers of those notes?"

"I think not. He only drew them from the bank the day before the accident. He was out with the hounds early next morning—he was engaged with his steward all the afternoon."

"We can get the numbers from the bank, I daresay," said the Colonel.

"True. But they will be of very little use to us. Bank-notes and diamonds are the bread and cheese of the burglar's trade. The thing is to find out who did this. I have an idea that I could put my hand upon the man—the hero of a good many portico robberies."

"Pray, what is a portico robbery?" asked the Colonel.

"Almost every country seat has a portico; the bigger the house the better the portico," explained the detective. "Nothing easier to scale than a handsome classical portico. No ladder or ropes, or tell-tale apparatus wanted. The burglar watches his opportunity, generally finds it at dusk, when the family are at dinner, the servants all occupied downstairs. He scales the portico—there is always at least one window above it. He gets quickly in at the window, sneaks along a corridor to my lady's dressing-room, or bed-room—of course he has learned the geography of the upper floor beforehand — finds her jewel-case, pitches it out of the window to friend or friends below — catch who catch can — and as quietly sneaks out of the house, and off to the nearest railway station, where friends have gone on before with trap. If he is met in the corridor after the fact, there is no property in his possession—he rushes past a bewildered maid-servant—gets clear off before she can collect her senses."

"And you think that this was a portico robbery?" said the Colonel.

"I know of only one man—a distinguished artist in that line—quick enough and audacious enough to manage this business in the time in which it was done," replied the detective. "Pray, Lady Darnel, how long were you absent from this room before you heard the pistol-shot?"

"A very short time."

"Five minutes?"

"Rather more than that—nearly ten minutes, perhaps."

"Ah! the man I mean could do a good deal more than ransack that cabinet in ten minutes. After you heard the pistol shot, did you lose much time in getting to this room?"

"Not an instant."

"And when you came in there was no one in the room but Sir Allan."

"No one."

"And you did not think of looking out of the window after the assassin."

"I thought of nothing but my husband."

"A pity. Yet I don't suppose you would have seen much if you had looked. Did nobody think of examining the grounds round the house that night?"

"No one," answered Colonel Stukely. "We ought to have hunted the scoundrel—but we were all half out of our wits. The only thought was of Sir Allan, and getting the doctor."

"So the man had his chance and got clean off. He must have left the neighbourhood by an early train, and got back to London. I daresay I shall be able to hear something about him at the station. By the way, Lady Darnel, do you remember if there was any conversation about those notes between you and Sir Allan that evening—anything that could have been overheard by a person standing outside the balcony."

"Sir Allan spoke of the notes before he put them away."

"Was the window open at the time?"

"Yes, there was a window open."

"Thank you, Lady Darnel, I don't think I need trouble you any more. Be kind enough to lock that cabinet, and keep the key in your possession. It is a good lock I suppose."

"It is a brahma lock, which Sir Allan had put on three years ago," said Dora.

Lady Darnel sank into her chair by the hearth, the pretty parti-coloured basket chair in which she had sat on many an evening chatting with her husband when the rest of the household had retired for the night. She sat with her hands idle in her lap, her eyes fixed and tearless, lost in painful thought. Yes, the notes were gone—and she knew too well whose hands had taken them. She could understand it all now, her son's persistent demand for three or four hundred pounds. He had been standing out on the balcony by the open window while Sir Allan talked about the notes; he had seen where they were put. He would have got them from her if he could, induced her to rob her husband for his benefit; it was towards that point he was urging when Grace's summons called her suddenly away, and he was left in the room with the money within his reach. Then came the diabolical temptation, an easy step from dishonourable dealing to absolute theft. The man who had never hesitated at cheating a creditor became in a moment the midnight robber. Then the surprise, the pistols lying there fatally ready for use, a shot fired at random, perhaps, and a hasty escape by the open window.

While she was thus picturing the horror of that night, Mr. Penwern was out in the balcony making a further investigation. A box of mignonette stood in his way as he stepped from the window to the balcony. It must have been in the way of the burglar in his flight. Mr. Penwern knelt down and examined the flowers and the mould under them. Yes, the man had trodden on the mignonette, there were broken stems, bruised leaves, and the deep print of a heel on one side of the box, a smallish heel, worn down on one side.

"A fashionably-made boot, but a dooced old boot," said Mr. Penwern to himself, as he studied that print in the mould. "I never knew Covey to sport any thing as shabby as that. Covey was always neat about his understandings. A man who has to get across country against time can't afford to be slipshod or down at heel."

The footprint in the mignonette-box made the manner of the burglar's escape a certainty to the mind of Mr. Penwern. He went downstairs with Colonel Stukely, and made a minute examination of the Italian garden in front of the balcony. He was able to trace footsteps in a diagonal line across the garden, deeply stamped upon flower-beds, and but faintly indicated here and there on the gravel-walks. The man had worn odd boots, one boot with a broader heel than the other, and a hole in the middle of the sole, both boots seemingly in the last stage of dilapidation.

"Egad," exclaimed the Colonel, after the detective had expatiated upon these marks, "he must have been a shabby devil."

As he spoke a sudden scare took hold of him. What if this man should have been the French adventurer, Grace's disreputable lover? The man he had seen lying on the common was clad like a tramp, shod like a tramp, and those indications on the flower-beds pointed to just such a man. Taking this fact in conjunction with Camillac's disappearance, his silence towards Grace, the Colonel felt that there was ground for fear. Unhappy Grace, if her folly should have brought this ruin upon her father's house.

And to pursue this investigation—which Penwern was conducting with ill-concealed cheerfulness, as of one certain of distinction and reward—to pursue this investigation to the end might be to inflict ineffable shame upon his god-daughter. Were this Camillac the offender, any trial, any public examination must needs bring that miserable episode of Grace's Parisian education into the broad glare of newspaper publicity. And the Colonel knew how charitable this world of the waning nineteenth century is, how given to look at the best and brightest side of a strange story, how loth to attribute evil to youth or womanhood. The Colonel saw his hazel-eyed darling's reputation blasted irretrievably in the very morning of life, he saw even honest Edward Colchester's faith uprooted, his love cast to the four winds. And in his heart Colonel Stukely cursed Dora Darnel for her officiousness.

Mr. Penwern seemed troubled in his mind after the discovery of those irregular prints in the flower-beds. He went back to them—he scrutinised them as closely as a great chemist might have watched some curious experiment. He was evidently dashed in spirits. He had made up his mind that this little affair had been carried through by the distinguished Covey. It bore, as he thought, the very stamp of Covey's workmanship; for Covey was unscrupulous, and would not have hesitated at shooting down anyone who came in his way. He did things neatly; but he did not mind a little blood now and then. But Mr. Penwern seemed to know Covey as if he were his brother, and he could not believe that any turn of fortune's wheel could bring Covey to wear such boots as those disgraceful objects that had left the print of their trodden-down heels on the flower-beds of Darnel.

"If I could believe in a tramp clever enough to do such neat work, I should say that this had been done by a tramp," said the detective, with conviction, "but I never knew a tramp yet that could rise above a kitchen-window robbery."

"Come back to the house and have some lunch," said the Colonel, with the sinister intent of giving the detective such liberal entertainment as should at least take the sharp edge off his perceptive faculties.

He could not hope to make such a respectable man drunk; but he thought it might be possible to get him slightly muddled.

Mr. Penwern was mortal, and Mr. Penwern was hungry. He had been travelling since half-past six o'clock, and it was now half-past twelve. The Darnel dining-room looked a very luxurious place after the refreshment-room at the Junction, where Mr. Penwern had regaled himself with a cup of tea, which had a strictly rustic flavour of new-mown hay, and a stale Bath bun. The Colonel urged Purdew in a confidential aside to do the very best he could for Mr. Penwern, and Purdew opined from the Colonel's tone that there was some especial reason for making much of the stranger. He sent a peremptory order to the kitchen, and he brought forth a fat cobwebby bottle of his choicest Burgundy, a velvetty Chambertin, with an aroma of violets. Beside this sacred wine, which reposed slanting-wise in a basket, the butler placed a pint decanter of a dry sherry, bright to the eye, pleasantly bitter to the taste, a tonic and an appetiser. The cook was quick to respond to the major-domo's order. In a little more than a quarter of an hour, just time enough for Mr. Penwern to look at Sir Allan's pictures and to wash his mouth out with a couple of glasses of the dry sherry—the meal was ready. A filletted sole with olives and mushrooms, a salmi of partridges, with plenty of truffles, in an incomparable sauce.

"This is the kind of thing I like," admitted Mr. Penwern, as he lapped up the sauce. He was not a man to put his knife in his mouth; but he unbent so far as to sop up the sauce with his bread. "This is the sort of snack I enjoy—something light and tasty. When I am on a job like this I usually find myself introduced to a cold sirloin, or a silver-side. People seem to think that nothing can be too substantial for Scotland Yard. Now I'm not an epicure, sir; but silver-sides and sirloins are apt to pall upon a man at my time of life. Thank you, sir, that Burgundy is the finest I ever partook of."

The detective had lunched luxuriously; and now he leant back in his chair, made himself thoroughly comfortable with his toothpick, and sipped the big bell-shaped glass of Burgundy.

"A very pleasant wine," he said approvingly; "a sound, wholesome wine."

"Don't be afraid of it, Mr. Penwern," said the Colonel, "it is too good a wine to do you any harm."

"Not after such a luncheon as I have partaken of," said the detective, who was evidently in an expansive mood. "A light little meal like that leaves a man's intellect free to work out a difficulty, whereas your cold sirloin and pickles weighs him down like lead, and your table-beer stupefies him. And yet in almost all the houses I go into it's the same old story, beef and beer. They forget, sir, that a man in my position can get beef and beer at home. He needn't go among the magnates of the land, and flog his brains in their service, for such entertainment as that. However, that's neither here nor there. What I have to do is to find the man who took those notes and fired that pistol."

"Don't you think that the odds are very much against your finding him, he having had three clear days' start?" suggested the Colonel.

"That increases the difficulty, I grant, sir; but it is a detective's business to rise superior to such difficulties. If it was Covey I should know where to put my hand upon him—but it's not Covey. Covey never wore down-at-heel boots, and Covey is much too clever to make a rush across flower-beds. Covey does his work clean, and leaves no slot behind him. I suppose the family will offer a handsome reward?"

"I really don't know. I think not," answered the Colonel nervously.

Mr. Penwern's countenance fell, in spite of the Burgundy.

"I don't think there's much chance of the man or the money being found unless the family offers a reward," said Penwern.

The door opened as he spoke. Dora Darnel entered quietly and took her seat near the Colonel, who would almost as soon have seen a cobra occupy those luxurious cushions.

"The family will offer a reward," said Dora, answering Mr. Penwern, who rose confusedly at her entrance, and began to fold his napkin, with a vague idea of getting it back into its original shape of a bishop's mitre. "I, on the part of my brother's family, will be answerable for the reward. Shall we offer a hundred pounds? Is that enough?"

"Hardly," replied Mr. Penwern. "The money stolen was four hundred. You had better offer two for the apprehension of the man who wounded

Sir Allan. If you get the man you are very likely to get back a part of the money."

"The money is of no consequence," said Dora, "but I do not wish my brother's murder—for it is too likely we may lose him—to go unavenged. We need not wait until he is dead to find the man who attempted his life."

"No, madam, there is not an hour to be lost. Time is half the battle in these cases," replied the detective.

He was flushed with meat and drink, his eyes sparkled, he had the comfortable look of a man who had lunched abundantly; but there was not the faintest indication of a muddled brain. Not a cloud overshadowed the professional intellect. Colonel Stukely felt that he and the cook and the butler had laboured in vain.

"With your permission, ma'am, I will go to the nearest town and get fifty small posters, offering the two-hundred pound reward," said the detective. "I can get 'em printed and distributed in a couple of hours, if I'm sharp."

"By all means," said Dora approvingly. "You can get a conveyance from the stable, and you had better make Darnel your headquarters while you are carrying on the investigation."

The Colonel got up suddenly, and walked out of the room in a savage humour. There could be no use in his wasting more time in diplomatic handling of the detective. The business was taken out of his hands. He could not offer Mr. Penwern three hundred pounds *not* to find the delinquent; and short of that he could do nothing. Stimulated by the offer of a reward the detective would bring his professional keenness into play at fullest power, while every loafer in the district would be on the alert to help him. Unless the man who did the deed had got clean off, and was already safe on the other side of the Channel, or on the high seas, there was little hope that he could escape the observation and inquiry that would be brought to bear upon his personality within the next few days. Wherever he was lurking there must be somebody to observe and to question him. Go where he will—be he a first-class traveller or a slip-shod tramp—the stranger is a mark for curiosity.

"It must be a race between the detective and me," the Colonel said to himself as he went in quest of Grace. "If the delinquent is the man I take him to be, I must find him and get him out of the country before this Scotland Yard vulture makes his swoop."

The evidence upon which Colonel Stukely had formed his conclusion was of the slightest. There were first those footprints, prints which he had examined as minutely as the detective himself. The marks of a small, narrow foot—a gentleman's foot—in a boot which, albeit worn to the quick, showed the lines of a fashionable maker. No hob-nailed Blucher, no ready-made Albert, ever left such an imprint. Secondly, there was the fact of Camillac's appearance in the neighbourhood of Darnel, in a condition which might inspire desperate acts; and then there came the fact of his evanishment without sign or token for Grace.

CHAPTER VIII.

"YET I MUST PROVE ALL TRUTH TO THEE."

THE Colonel found his god-daughter in her own little sitting-room, very unhappy, utterly unable to employ herself. Lady Darnel was in the next room. She would not allow Grace to remain with her. She preferred to be alone.

"She does nothing but brood, and I do nothing but brood," said Grace, who came out into the corridor to talk to the Colonel. "If we go on much longer like this we shall both be in a lunatic asylum."

The Colonel patted her gently on the shoulder, but could offer no better consolation. He had talked very confidentially with the doctor on the previous evening, and he had little hope of his old comrade's recovery.

"Your Aunt Dora is active enough for the whole household," he said bitterly.

"She is positively diabolical," exclaimed Grace. "The idea of her sending for a detective, and worrying poor Lady Darnel with questions about that wretched money, as if it could do my dear father any good to find the burglar who shot him. Of course, I should like the wretch to be hanged, but I can't think of him or anything else till my dearest father is out of danger."

"I am going for a prowl, Grace. I shan't wait for luncheon, as I want a long afternoon."

"The house is just a shade drearier when you are out of it," said Grace, with a sigh.

"You have not had any letter or message from Mr. Camillac?"

"Not a word. I feel convinced that he is dead—that he died of cold and hunger under some hedge; but I feel as if it didn't matter. I daresay I shall feel sorry for him by-and-by when my father is out of danger."

"I don't suppose he is dead, Grace. A man of that age is not so easily killed."

"If he were not dead or dying, I should have heard of him before now," said Grace, with conviction. "Why did he come to this place except to see me? He was penniless, and he knows that I am rich. What more natural than that he should appeal to me? He could not go on existing without money."

"No, he could not go on without money," thought the Colonel.

The whole story seemed clear to him. This Camillac had been lurking about the grounds that night with the hope of seeing Grace. He saw the lighted windows of Lady Darnel's room, opening upon a balcony which was easy to climb —he scaled the balcony, overheard Sir Allan's talk about the bank-notes, saw where they were put and made a rush for them when the room was empty. The whole transaction had grown out of the inspiration of the moment—an unpremeditated crime, suggested by opportunity. He had come to the house to get a few pounds from his sweetheart; and he had suddenly seen a chance of helping himself to four hundred.

And now, for Grace's sake, the Colonel wanted to get this scoundrel out of the way at any cost to himself of trouble or hard cash. He was not a poor man, and he could afford to spare a few hundreds for his favourite. The difficulty was where to find the man. If he had got clear off out of the clutches of the law it was well, and he might riot upon his ill-gotten gains at a distance without inflicting evil upon Grace; but if he were in hiding anywhere within thirty miles of Darnel, the odds were that he would fall into the hands of Mr. Penwern, and the whole story would come to light at the next quarter sessions.

The Colonel rode slowly down the avenue on his old bay cob, a cob that was the very essence of sobriety and good manners as a hack, and yet when inspired by a view-halloa and good company could go at a tremendous pace in a burst across country. He rode very slowly, meditating where and how he was to pursue his quest of Mr. Camillac. He had already visited almost every cottage, and explored every copse and common in the neighbourhood.

Half-way down the avenue he met Edward Colchester on foot.

"I was just going up to the house to make an enquiry," he said. "Any improvement in Sir Allan since the morning?"

The Colonel shook his head.

"Friedricson is to be here to-morrow," he said; "and if the bullet can be extracted then there may be some hope. But just at present things look very bad."

"Poor Grace," said Colchester. "How sad it is for her. I should like to go and talk to her a bit, if you think I shouldn't be a nuisance."

"I am sure you would not be a nuisance, and your society would do Grace good. She is in a wretched state, poor girl. If you hurry up to the house you'll find them at lunch, and Grace can hardly refuse to see you," said the Colonel, who was a secret ally of Monsieur de Camillac's rival.

"A thousand thanks!" exclaimed the young squire, starting off at a run.

The family were at luncheon. Mr. Colchester asked to be shown into the dining-room, determined not to be relegated to the solitude of the drawing-room, and to a formal interview with Dora. They could not turn him away from their table in a house famous for hospitality; and, however dismal the meal might be, it would be rapture—a sad kind of rapture, of course—to sit by Grace in sympathetic silence, and admire the outline of cheek and throat, the little rings of auburn hair which clustered in the hollow of her neck, the heavy coil of plaits, the gracious contour of her head.

Dora Darnel and her niece were seated at opposite ends of the table, as far apart as they could be. Grace sat with an empty plate before her, the image of despair. She gave a wan smile when Mr. Colchester came in and took his seat by her side, uninvited, except by the servant who laid a cover for him.

"How very good of you to come again," said Dora, with a faint emphasis on the last word.

"I hope you don't mind my coming so often. No, not any lunch, thank you," to the servant. "But I really could not rest without looking round again. I have to dine at Mawlesford to-night, Sir Roger Brandon's, don't you know—a nine-mile drive, a horrid bore. I don't feel a bit in the cue for going out. This—this sad business has upset me more than I can say."

Grace lifted those heavy eyelids of hers, and gave him a grateful look out of her soft brown eyes: such luminous eyes they had been in the days of her gladness; but to Edward Colchester they seemed even lovelier in sorrow. That soft appealing look went straight to his heart.

Yes, she was glad to see him. She had been living in an awful solitude of grief and fear—fearing her father's death, fearing for her lover, that lover of whose existence she could not think without a shudder. Oh, the folly of those Parisian days—the silly romance, the fatuity of it all! What a burden she had laid upon herself—what a chain she had forged for her young life. If this faithful admirer of hers, who looked up to her with such respectful devotion, if he could know how idiotic she had been, how must his admiration be changed to scorn, his regard to loathing. It was the thought of this which made her uncivil to him. She wanted to keep him at arm's length, if possible. She would not give him reason to reproach her for hypocrisy and double-dealing.

But to-day in the utter desolation of her life she turned involuntarily to this friend of her childhood. How good and true he was, how frank, and honest, and straightforward. Not so elegant, not so accomplished or fascinating as Victor de Camillac; but what a thoroughbred English gentleman, without fear or reproach—a man to stand before kings and not be ashamed.

"Is Lady Darnel too ill to come down to lunch?" enquired Mr. Colchester.

"She is not ill—but she is very miserable, poor thing," answered Grace.

"And she gives way to her grief," said Dora; "I always envy the people who give way to their grief. They generally get over it so soon."

"I do not think Lady Darnel will get over her grief very soon, Aunt Dora, if my father is taken away from us," said Grace, with a stifled sob.

"How pale you are looking," said Edward Colchester. "I don't believe you have had any fresh air since this trouble began. Will you come for a turn on the terrace; it is a lovely afternoon?"

"Yes," said Grace, rising suddenly, "I will come. I think I should go mad if I stayed in this house any longer. I must go upstairs and hear the last report of my father, and then I will go for a ramble in the garden. You'll come, Aunt Dora?"

"No, Grace; I shall not leave the house. I can exist without fresh air."

Grace looked embarrassed, but having accepted Mr. Colchester's invitation she could not recede all at once. The withdrawal would be too marked. She went away, and came back in about ten minutes with a white Shetland shawl wrapped round her shoulders.

"There is no change in the sick-room," she said. "It is always the same answer—no change—no improvement. Oh, those nurses, what machines they are! I wonder if they seem a little more human when their own people are ill? Come, Mr. Colchester."

She went out to the terrace, walking very quickly in her nervous agitation. It was an infinite relief to feel the fresh autumnal breeze blowing over her face and hair, to breathe in a wider space. It seemed to her as if it were weeks since she had felt that cool reviving air and looked across that wide expanse of lawn to the wider region of oaks and beeches which had been the fairy forest of her childhood fancies. Through just such a wood Red Riding Hood had gone unconscious to her doom. Through just such a wood Fatima's brothers had ridden to the rescue of Bluebeard's last victim. In just such a wood Beauty had dwelt meekly in the Palace of the enchanted Beast; in just such a wood she had bent over the dying monster, breathing soft words of pity into his ear, and had seen him restored to the grace and glory of manhood, the perfect Prince of Fairyland. With all her heart Grace loved the domain that had been her cradle and her playground.

It was a delicious afternoon, the low sun golden above the undulating line of beeches, with their rounded crests dark against the glowing sky, wave above wave, billowy masses of dark verdure soon to be touched with the varied hues of decay.

For a little while Grace and her companion walked about the lawn in silence, she too unhappy to speak, he racking his brain for something appropriate, or at least an inoffensive subject of conversation.

"How well the shrubberies are looking," he said at last, feeling as if the remark were a flash of inspiration.

Now the shrubberies had been Sir Allan's

peculiar pride. He had filled them with new and rare conifers, with every variety of flowering shrubs; under his supervision they had been fed with the most scientific preparations that can enrich the soil, they had been watched, and sheltered from the frost, and cared for as if they had been precious human things.

"Yes, they are too lovely," said Grace. "I never saw that picea nobilis look so superb as it does this year. My father is so proud of it. And to think that he may never see those trees again!"

Here she began to cry, and again Edward Colchester felt that he was a brute. He seemed predestined to say brutish things, to put his finger-tip upon open wounds.

He walked by her side while she dried her tears, his heart aching for her, his love flowing out towards her like a magnetic stream. They were in one of the winding shrubbery paths, which they two had trodden many a time, gaily, carelessly, as comrades and playfellows, in those remote days before his friendly feeling for a pretty girl had ripened into passionate love, before trouble or care had darkened her young life. It was a path completely screened by conifers and evergreens, out of sight of the house. In a forest they could not have been more alone. At the end of the path there was a little Swiss chalet, a fantastic summer-house of carved wood, in which Mr. Colchester had often had five o'clock tea after a warm afternoon at lawn-tennis. It was Grace's favourite retreat in fine weather, and her books and drawing materials were scattered on the rustic table just as she had left them a week ago. She looked at them with a listless air, and stopped to put the books together.

"Fifine, Maud, La Petite Fadette," she said as she gathered up the volumes. "How happy was that last morning I sat here reading. Such a warm morning—like July. Everything was so lovely, the air so delicious. I forgot that I had a care."

"What care could you have to forget a week ago?" asked Colchester.

"Oh, there are cares in every life. Everybody has some kind of burden to carry. But I never knew what real sorrow meant till my father's life was in danger."

Her tears flowed afresh at the thought of that peril, and then Edward Colchester forgot himself altogether, and caught her in his arms, and kissed the sad, tear-stained face again and again.

"My beloved, let me share your grief, let me be all in all to you in your day of sorrow. My dearest, you know how fondly I love you."

It was all done in a moment. She was in

his arms, his beloved, accepting his devotion, the passive recipient of betrothal kisses, for such kisses could mean nothing less than betrothal. They were the first lover's kisses that had ever touched her lips. Never before had she felt the passionate pulse of a lover's heart beating against her own. She tore herself from his arms.

"How can you, how can you!" she cried reproachfully. "To talk of love when my father lies on his death-bed! I know they all believe it is his death-bed. I hate you for such heartlessness."

"Gracie, is it heartless to adore you, to want to comfort you in your sorrow?" he asked reproachfully. "I have been quietly worshipping you for a year; waiting, waiting, for some sign of awakening love on your part. I should not have dared to speak even yet: only to see you in tears and not to be able to comfort you was too much."

"You cannot comfort me. I am full of trouble," she answered passionately.

She had flung her books upon the table, and had left the chalet hurriedly, and was walking quickly along the path that led to the house. He felt that she was angry with him—that he had, as it were, violated the sanctity of her sorrow—and yet he believed himself her accepted lover. For one delicious moment she had rested in his arms, her eyes had looked at him, not in anger, but in answering love. Those lips of hers had yielded themselves to his kisses. He knew that she loved him—that he had but to wait for a more fitting time to press his suit. And he had her father upon his side, the good old Colonel too. He had fortune, youth, everything that makes fitness in union. And he knew of no likely rival. Could he doubt that he should win her? His heart glowed with triumph as he hurried after her swift footsteps, overtook her, and stood at her side.

"Forgive me, Grace. I will wait for a happier day," he said.

"That day will never come for you and me," she answered coldly. "Pray forget that you have been so foolish, as I shall try to do."

"Forget those kisses? Never! Grace, I will not be put off like this. I will wait. I will not even speak of my love until your father is out of danger—but you must not thrust me from you coldly; you must not deny my right to claim you by and by."

"Never, never, never," she said. "I tell you it can never be."

"Then you do not love me," he cried, seizing her hands, holding her there on the path, face to face with him, beside himself with love and anger. "You were deceiving me just now, or I was mad and deceived myself. You do not care a straw for me. Say that, Grace—only say that you don't care for me, and you shall never see my face again."

She could not say it; not for the life of her could she so belie her beating heart, which had gone out to him as a bird to its nest, which belonged to him as a slave to her master.

"I cannot engage myself to you," she said. "There are reasons."

"What reasons? There can be no reason except that you detest me. Why not say so at once, and make an end of the matter? If there were obstacles I would overcome them. Give me one grain of love—no bigger than a mustard seed—and I would remove mountains. But there are no obstacles. We have everything on our side. Your father likes me—he was my father's dearest friend—he would like to see us married."

"I can never marry you," said Grace sadly. "Why do you press me with painful questions? Please let go my hands."

He released her instantly, with a gloomy look.

"I see. There is someone else whom you love better," he said.

"No, there is no one," she said impetuously, and then repented that she had so spoken.

"Grace, you are a mystery. If you would only say that you hate me——"

"I will not tell a lie," she answered, walking on towards the house, he still by her side. "If you have any compassion for my present unhappiness you will say no more."

"Then I will say no more. I know I am a brute—an utterly brutish brute. I suppose having behaved so badly, I must not come to Darnel any more."

"You can do as you like about that," she answered wearily.

"Then I shall come. Life would be a burden if I could not see you now and then."

In her heart of hearts she liked to see him; for her life would have been a blank without that pleasant companionship. She had snubbed him unmercifully ever since her return from Paris, and yet he had never wavered in his devotion. And he had his reward, though he knew it not; for he had won her in spite of herself. But she was a true Darnel, and had a loyal regard for a promise once given. And in an evil hour she had given a promise which bound her to Victor de Camillac or to life-long celibacy.

"Good-bye," she said curtly, and Mr. Colchester was fain to accept his dismissal.

They were close to the hall door by this time. He had no excuse for lingering any longer.

"Good-bye, Grace—my Grace," he said, with a final flash of determination.

And then as he walked slowly down the avenue he repeated to himself, "My Grace, mine; yes, my dear, mine, for I mean to win you."

He was sorely troubled in mind as he walked back to the Manor through those rural Wiltshire lanes, with their tall, tangled hedgerows.

That severer order of agriculture which cuts down hedges to the quick, absorbs waste places, and uproots the timber of centuries, had not yet spoiled the Manor. Mr. Colchester's farmers were content to be slovenly and picturesque, as their fathers and grandfathers had been before them, under the sway of the easiest of landlords.

He went home full of trouble and perplexity. There had been that in Grace's eyes, as she looked upon him, which seemed to him an assurance of her love. There had been that in the sweet mouth, with lips half-parted and faintly tremulous, which told of deepest feeling. For some blissful moments he had held her in his arms, flushed with triumph, believing himself her accepted lover. And then she had thrust him from her, and told him that she could never be his wife. There was a contradiction here that argued a mystery, a mystery in the life of a girl who had been to him as the incarnation of purity and truth. If she could deceive, if she could stoop to double-dealing, there was an end of Edward Colchester's faith in womanhood.

CHAPTER IX.

"I LOVE, AND HE LOVES ME AGAIN."

COLONEL STUKELY spent a long and wearisome afternoon dawdling about the lanes and little clusters of labourers' cottages which called themselves villages, entering into conversation with every man, woman, and child whom he could beguile into a dialogue, and suffering intensely from his conscientious efforts to understand a patois which was almost as a foreign language to him. In this wise, performing the part of the benevolent friend of humanity, a character partaking the idiosyncrasies of Haroun Alraschid and Sir Roger de Coverley, he heard much irrelevant matter, from village politics and pot-house philosophy to the smallest domestic details, with the full, true, and particular account of the speaker's latest "stand-further" with the Squire, the Parson, or the bailiff. But in all the flood of talk to which he listened with a sublime patience the good Colonel could discover not one solitary sentence bearing upon the task which he had set himself to perform.

Riding slowly homewards he tried to cheer himself with the notion that as he had failed in the endeavour to trace the footsteps of Victor Camillac, so also must Mr. Penwern fail. He had no apprehension that his talents in the detective line were inferior to those of the professional enquirer. Indeed, it seemed to him that his education and experience must be more than a match for the technical training of Scotland Yard. He argued, therefore, that the young Frenchman had got clear off, and that he had nothing to fear for his beloved god-daughter.

The eight o'clock dinner was a dismal function. Lady Darnel still kept her room. Miss Darnel sat in her brother's place and went through the ceremonial with a fortitude which savoured of martyrdom. Grace edged her chair as close as she could to the Colonel's, ate hardly anything, and was curiously absent-minded, looking up at her godfather every now and then with a little appealing glance that went straight to his heart smiling to herself now and then, as she looked down at her plate, with a strange shy smile, and at one stage of the entertainment suddenly bursting into tears.

"My dear Grace, if you cannot command yourself better than this, you should follow Lady Darnel's example, and hide yourself from the light of day," remonstrated her aunt.

"Let her cry," said the Colonel, patting the girl's shoulder affectionately. "Tears are a comfort sometimes; and why should she repress the signs of her grief? There is no secret about her sorrow. We are all of the same mind."

The Colonel had no inclination to sit alone over his claret. He left the dining-room with Miss Darnel and her niece. In the hall Grace put her arm through his.

"Come on the terrace for a little walk," she said.

"My dear Grace, there is no moon, and it is very cold," urged Dora. "What pleasure can there be in walking on the terrace on such a night?"

"No pleasure. I do not expect pleasure, but I must have air. I am stifling for want of air."

"I should have thought you had air enough this afternoon when you were tearing about the grounds with Mr. Colchester," retorted her aunt sharply.

"Will you come, godpapa?" asked Grace, ignoring the reproof. "You don't mind walking up and down the terrace with me for a quarter of an hour, even if it is dark and cold."

"I shall like it very much, if you put on your jacket."

Grace ran upstairs, obtained the last bulletin of her father's condition—always the same hopeless report — and came down in her sealskin jacket. In another minute she and the Colonel were out of doors, and beyond the searching eye and the keen ear of Dora. The night was moonless, but not altogether dark. The stars were shining above the tree tops in the park, a dense rampart of foliage which shut out the world beyond.

"Any news?" asked Grace excitedly, hanging on the Colonel's arm.

"Not a word. I believe that unlucky young fellow has got clear off; and you may wash your hands of him and his fate."

"I cannot do that," said Grace gloomily; "I am under a promise."

"No promise can hold good with a criminal," answered the Colonel.

"A criminal! In heaven's name, what do you mean?"

"I mean that a detective has been at Darnel this morning, and that he has discovered the footprints of a stranger across the flower-beds, just such footprints as would be made by that wretched down-at-heel creature we saw on the common. There was a considerable sum of money stolen out of Lady Darnel's morning-room, money which we all know to have been there on the night your father was shot. It is clear to the man from Scotland Yard that Sir Allan was wounded by a stranger who entered that room and stole that money. Now, my reading of the story is, that this Camillac was hanging about the house on that night, in the hope of getting an interview with you, that he was on the balcony for some time, saw the money put away, and took advantage of Lady Darnel's leaving the room to enter and possess himself of that money. He was surprised by your father, and turned upon him—in the manner we know."

"No, no; it is too horrible! The man I once loved, the man I promised to marry—a midnight robber—a murderer! It cannot be," protested Grace. "Surely I am not an utter fool. I know that man was a gentleman by birth, a gentleman by education and breeding."

"Gentlemen drift to the gutter; gentlemen join the criminal classes every day in the year, my poor Grace," said the Colonel gravely. "I do not suppose for a moment that you would mistake a cad for a gentleman; but there is such a thing as a reckless man gone thoroughly to the bad; and I'm afraid your Victor de Camillac is just such an one. All we can hope is that he has got clear off, and that your dear father's wound may not prove fatal."

"Fatal! Oh, God, if it were, I should be my father's murderer—for it was my folly that brought that man to this house. Oh, why should so trivial a sin bring such a terrible punishment? If my father were to die I should never lift up my head again. I should pray God to end my days. I never, never could know peace of mind any more!"

She clung to her kind old friend, sobbing hysterically, beside herself with horror.

"My dear child, don't give way to such grief," said the Colonel soothingly. "God grant your father may recover. And, after all, this suspicion of mine may be wrong. The criminal may be a stranger of whom we know nothing. Remember it is only a conjecture on my part."

"If you were right, if it were he, my sin would have been the cause of my father's death," said Grace, and then she remembered that bitter cry of Lady Darnel's, those awful words spoken by the lips of a sleeper, "My fault, my fault! I murdered him!"

How strange that those self-accusing words, uttered unconsciously, should be echoed now by Grace, waking and sentient.

"No, I will not believe it," she said presently. "After all, there is no evidence to go upon. There is no real ground for such a hideous suspicion. I believe that poor creature fell down somewhere ill or dying, and that he never came to Darnel Park."

"You may be right, Grace. My view of the case was only a succession of conjectures. I should never have thought of it if that man from Scotland Yard had not set my wits at work. There is something infectious in the manœuvres of these people. Only I thought it right to tell you everything, more especially as you insist upon considering yourself bound to this adventurer."

"I insist upon acting as a woman of honour should act," answered Grace, with a heroic air. "You men are always talking about honour as if it were a peculiar property of your sex. You pretend to think that we poor weak things don't even know what it means. Now I want you to understand that you are guilty of scandalous injustice. *Eine Frau ein Wort.*"

"And you consider yourself bound to a beggar."

"I consider myself bound to him till he releases me. I know he would release me from my promise, if I could only see him and tell him everything."

"Indeed! There is something that he must be told then?"

"Yes," murmured Grace, hanging her pretty head.

Colonel Stukely lifted the bent head between his hands, and kissed his god-daughter's forehead.

"My pet, I begin to understand," he said. "I suspected all through that dreary dinner that you had something to tell me. You have found out at last that a frank honest young fellow whom you have known since childhood is better worth loving than an unknown foreigner whom you met by chance in a picture gallery."

"Mr. Colchester was walking in the shrubbery with me this afternoon," faltered Grace, "and he asked me to be his wife. It was very, very sudden; and he took me so by surprise that I'm afraid I allowed him to think that I am rather fond of him."

"What was it you said, Grace?"

"It was not anything I said to him. It was only my manner."

"Oh," said the Colonel. "It was your manner, was it? There is a good deal in manner. And I suppose by the time you left the shrubbery you had engaged yourself to young Colchester, in spite of your promise to the Frenchman. This is your view of *eine Frau ein Wort*, I take it. One at a time."

"You insist upon your mean opinion of me," cried Grace, stamping her foot. "No, I did not engage myself to Mr. Colchester. I told him that I could never marry him. I tried to tell him that I did not care for him, but my lips would not speak the false words. I know now that I do care for him, that the other was only a foolish infatuation, of which I have good reason to be ashamed."

"I am glad you have found out the truth at last, Grace. Now, my darling, you mustn't fret any more. Leave everything to Providence and your old godfather. Hark! there are wheels coming up the avenue. Who can it be at such an hour? The doctor paid his last visit before dinner."

It was Mr. Penwern in a fly from the village. Colonel Stukely hurried back to the house, dreading, yet eager, to hear the detective's account of his investigations. Mr. Penwern was shown into the library, where the Colonel found him closeted with Dora Darnel, who had not lost a minute in going to him.

"Well, Mr. Penwern, what's your news?" asked the Colonel, taking the case out of Dora's hands.

The detective had an idea that the money and the authority were both on the side of the lady;

but there was that in the Afghan hero's bearing and tone which could not be slighted.

"My afternoon has not been unprofitable," answered Penwern. "I have got the bills out—fifty of them—and I believe I am on the right track for the man."

"Indeed," said the Colonel, feeling very uncomfortable.

He had an intense dread of publicity for that little episode of Grace's schoolgirl life, a dread which was intensified by the circumstance of Colchester's proposal.

"Yes, I think I am on the right scent this time. The bills had an immediate effect. Most people had heard of Sir Allan's wound, but the robbery of the notes was news to everybody. I distributed the bills with my own hands, and the villagers at whose shops I left them had all a good deal to say about the trouble at the great house. The old woman who keeps a general shop—grocery, clothes, boots——"

"Mrs. Mopp," said Dora.

"Mrs. Mopp. Yes, that's the lady. She insisted on my helping her to spell through the bill from beginning to end. When she came to the part about the notes she became tremendously excited. 'I wouldn't mind laying a wager it was that scoundrel did it,' she said. 'What scoundrel?' asked I. 'Jaker,' said she; and she had such a rooted idea that I ought to know all about Mr. Jaker that I could hardly induce her to tell me anything about him."

"He is a very disreputable person," said Dora, looking up at the Colonel, "a poacher; a man who has been in prison more times than anyone can remember. He lives half in and half out of prison. People are very kind to his wretched wife and children, who are always in a state of semi-starvation. But last year he turned savage and set himself deliberately to annoy Mr. Colchester and the hunting men. He shot a number of foxes, and waylaid the hunting people when they were drawing the covers, and used most abominable language, and since then he has been altogether an outlaw, and his family are allowed to starve. It is considered an offence against every member of the hunt to give them so much as a loaf of bread."

"Not a man likely to be changing a twenty-pound note, honestly come by," said the detective.

"Do you mean to say that Jaker has been changing twenty-pound notes?"

"He changed one at eight o'clock yesterday morning, at Mrs. Mopp's shop, where he bought himself a regular rig-out—boots, corduroy suit, flannel shirts, pilot overcoat, sou'-wester. Mrs.

Mopp had not done so big a line for years, she told me. He made her rout him out an old tea chest to carry his kit, and walked off with it to Scadleigh station, in time for the nine o'clock train to London. He told nobody where he was going; but there is an idea that he meant Canada."

"He has often talked of Canada, and the great things he could do there," said Miss Darnel. "I have heard as much from his wife, whom I used to visit at one time."

"Before her husband put himself out of court by shooting foxes," remarked the Colonel, with a sudden air of cheerfulness which deeply offended Dora.

It was such an inexpressible relief to him to see the detective on an entirely new scent, that he for the moment forgot the cloud of sorrow brooding over the house of Darnel.

"I paid Mrs. Jaker a visit this evening," said the detective. "I was surprised to find what roomy quarters your poor have to starve in. Why, in London a house as big as Jaker's cottage would be made to accommodate forty people. The cubical contents of the pigstye are more than those of a room that lodges a family in Whitechapel."

"It is an old homestead that once went with a small farm," explained Dora. "When the land was taken away to join to the next farm the old cottage remained empty for some years. And then it was let cheap to Jaker, who was not quite such a bad character in those days. I don't suppose he has paid any rent for the last ten years; but the cottage is in an out-of-the-way place, and would not suit everybody."

"I should think not, indeed, ma'am," said the detective, shuddering. "I never saw such a cut-throat place. The cottage is at the end of a long lane, ankle deep in mud, which leads to nowhere."

"It is an accommodation lane," remarked Dora.

"Lord knows whom it can be intended to accommodate, ma'am. The cottage is half a mile from any other house, and how any Christian in his sober senses could be tempted to go there, except from motives of benevolence, is more than I understand. However, I found my way there this evening—in the dark, too—and a nice state my boots were in when I got there. I had to go back to the inn and get myself brushed up before I could venture to show myself here. But I saw Mrs. Jaker, and I put her through a pretty close catechism; and I don't think there's any doubt that, in consequence of the telegram I sent to Scotland Yard this morning, Mr. Jaker will be stopped at Liverpool before he can get on board the vessel that was to take him to Canada."

"You believe he means to try for Canada?" enquired the Colonel.

"From what I got out of Mrs. Jaker I don't think there's the slightest doubt of it."

"Mrs. Jaker is a very artful person," said Miss Darnel. "I know she has always contrived to deceive *me*."

The detective smiled quietly, and to himself as it were. He could not see that this fact had any bearing on the case. It was one thing to hoodwink a spinster brought up in cotton-wool; it was another thing to deceive a man educated in Scotland Yard.

"Did you find out whether Jaker has left his wife any of the money?"

"He may have left her a pound or two to keep the wolf from the door till he chooses to send her the passage-money for herself and her children. They were swarming about the place like rabbits in a warren, poor little beggars. He promises to send for her directly he gets there, and has looked about him a bit. I don't believe she has any idea of a robbery, or of his being possessed of a large sum of money. He told her that he had won ten pounds at Shiveram races, putting five shillings on a horse that stood at forty to one in the betting. She believed him, poor soul, though it was a puzzle to her to know where he got the five shillings. And it's my belief he has left her to starve, or to live upon charity till he chooses to send her the passage-money."

"You don't know Mrs. Jaker," said Dora. "From what *I* know of her character I should say she knows all about the robbery, and has the lion's share of the money in her possession."

"Do you really think so?" said the detective, with a troubled look. "If I thought that I'd get a magistrate's warrant to-morrow morning and search the house; but she looked to me such a weak, helpless, trodden-down creature."

"That's all acting. When Jaker annoyed the hunting men she used to go with him, and her language was worse than his. Mr. Colchester said it was she who goaded him on to do it."

"I'll get a warrant to-morrow morning," said Mr. Penwern.

"You must have a good appetite for supper after such a laborious afternoon and evening," said the Colonel. "Will you order something for Mr. Penwern, Miss Darnel?"

He rang the bell, and Dora informed the footman who answered it that Mr. Penwern would take supper in the housekeeper's room. This was a fall almost as big as Wolsey's, after the elegant little luncheon with which Mr. Penwern had been regaled at the Colonel's bidding. "So like a maiden aunt," thought the detective, as he went off through long corridors and winding ways to that humbler and busier portion of the mansion, which was as the old town of Edinburgh to the new town. In this more lowly quarter, however, he was well cared for, and contrived to spend a jovial evening.

CHAPTER X.

"A POWER OF HELL O'ERCLOUDS THY UNDERSTANDING."

As an old campaigner, Colonel Stukely found no difficulty in awaking at any hour of the morning at which he wished to rise. He needed to victimise no servant who must rise still earlier to call him—nor did he require to have his courage stimulated by a cup of hot tea. He went to his bedroom directly the detective had retired to the servants' quarters, and he told himself as he lay down to rest that he would be astir at half-past four o'clock next morning; not with any idea of cub-hunting, but with the serious intention of getting an interview with Mrs. Jaker before detective or search-warrant could reach her cottage. Before bidding Miss Darnel good-night he had contrived to ascertain from that lady the exact situation of the cottage. It lay within a mile of the park gates, in a particularly lonely district, given over to agriculture. Half-a-dozen small farms had been rolled into one, and the homesteads belonging to them had been pulled down or turned into labourers' cottages. The Jakers' domicile was situated at the end of a long lane, just where the uttermost limit of cultivated land met the edge of a wild stretch of common. It had been a homestead in the time of the Stuarts, and had a picturesque air even now, in the lowest stage of neglect and decay, the rotten and ragged thatch half hidden under a goodly growth of weeds and grasses, the good old leaded lattices with hardly a whole pane among them. The Jakers were squatters rather than tenants, and would have been turned out neck and crop years ago had it not been for an easy-going landlord and the little peculiarities of Mrs. Jaker, who always had a baby at hand at the hour of any financial crisis. It was sometimes a baby that moment born—anon a baby that very morning dead. Living or dead the baby was always ready for the emergency. It was Mrs. Jaker's ace of trumps.

Having told himself that he should be astir at half-past four, the Colonel woke a few minutes before the hour. He had scarcely sounded his repeater when the eight-day clock in the corridor chimed in with its four musical notes, and then its four sonorous strokes upon the big bell. The Colonel was up and in his bath within five minutes. Not a man he to yawn and loiter, and think twice about leaving his pillow, when there was business to be done.

It was pitch dark as yet—it would hardly be light by the time he should arrive at Mrs. Jaker's cottage; but he calculated that a person of her condition would be an early riser, and he felt no compunction about knocking her up should she prove a slug-a-bed. He was bent upon seeing her before the detective arrived with his search-warrant; so that in the event of her husband having obtained his plunder from Victor de Camillac the woman's mouth might be sealed as to the existence and whereabouts of that obnoxious Frenchman.

"My friend Penwern ignores those foot-marks on the flower-beds now that he has started on another track," the Colonel thought, as he walked briskly along the avenue under the cold October sky. "Not very logical. That narrow sole and pointed heel could never have belonged to the boot of a rustic poacher; and yet those foot-marks have to be accounted for somehow, and I am not at all clear that Grace's admirer is safe out of the business."

Before going downstairs the Colonel had tapped softly at his friend's door, and had questioned the night nurse. Her reply was more favourable than usual. The patient had spent a quieter night, the temperature was a little lower, the delirium less violent. All this was hopeful.

There were patches of gray in the eastern sky by the time the Colonel came to the end of the long muddy lane, and entered Mrs. Jaker's neglected garden. The gate hung loose upon broken hinges, and several of its rails had been ruthlessly plucked off to serve for firewood. The palings were in the same condition, and afforded free access to vagabond swine. When Mrs. Jaker was asked why she did not keep her garden tidy, she replied that tidiness was impossible while the pigs came in and uprooted every thing; but when she was asked why she and her husband did not patch up the palings and keep the pigs out, Mrs. Jaker became desperate, and asked if pales dropped from the skies, and if Providence showered nails and hammers into poor people's laps. For her part she had neither wood, nor nails, nor hammer; and as for the landlord, he would see them all dead before he would do anything for them. This could scarcely be considered strange, inasmuch as they did nothing for him in the shape of rent.

Albeit the sky was gray in the east, and a faint admixture of silvery light glorified the undulating lines of hill and woodland. Mrs. Jaker had not yet left her pillow when the Colonel knocked with his stout oak stick at the cottage door. She put her head out of an upstair window presently, however, and on hearing that he had particular business with her, promised to be down in ten minutes. So the Colonel strolled up and down the dreary little garden, with its stagnant puddles in depressed corners and its ragged regiment of barren cabbage-stalks, and seeing at least half an acre of ground given over to desolation, he wondered how it was that the country poor made so little of their opportunities.

The cottage door opened while he stood at gaze above the cabbage stalks, and he was admitted to the Jaker abode. Mrs. Jaker's toilet was of the briefest, and the Colonel could not help suspecting that she had slept in her gown. A swarm of healthy, handsome children, all in the last stage of rags and dirt, were squatting and scrambling about the wide hearth, which had evidently belonged to the farm-house kitchen. The few sticks of furniture were all in a ruinous condition; and it was not without careful selection that Mrs. Jaker found a chair which she could venture to offer to her guest. When he had seated himself she knelt on the hearth and lighted a fire of sticks and turf which made a cheerful flare of light amidst the greyness of early morning. While she was doing this she turned her head now and then and looked timidly and interrogatively at the Colonel. She was scared by the appearance of a stranger at this unwonted hour; but she was accustomed to be visited from time to time by the "gentry," who came to remonstrate with her upon her own and her husband's misdoings.

"You had a stranger here last night, Mrs. Jaker," began the Colonel.

"Yes, sir, there was a person here."

"Exactly. I know all about him and what passed. You have not heard the last of that person and his enquiries. It would have been wiser if you had told him the truth about that money which is to pay your husband's passage to Canada, and set you all up in a new country. It is a nice little fortune for a man like Jaker to drop into. It ought to buy him a pretty little farm out yonder."

Mrs. Jaker paled at this speech, and a frightened look came into those mild blue eyes of hers, eyes which were apt to mislead strangers as to her character.

"Fortune, sir!" she faltered. "My poor husband had nothing but the ten pound he won at the races."

"Indeed! Then how came he to spend nearly ten pounds with the old woman at the shop? That would leave him very little for his passage money."

Hereupon Mrs. Jaker, with tears in her eyes, called upon the heavens and those who dwell therein to witness her truth. She had told the strange gentleman who called last night the truth, and nothing but the truth. If her husband had more money than those ten sovereigns won for him by the horse True Blue—which was a Wiltshire-bred horse and well beknown to him, or Jaker would never have backed him—she knew it not.

"Come now, Mrs. Jaker, this is all very foolish," said the Colonel, in a friendly tone. "Suppose I were to tell you that the person you saw last night is coming again this morning, and that in all probability he will take you off to prison. A man in Jaker's station doesn't come by four hundred pounds in bank-notes without people asking questions, and as Jaker has made off it will be for you to answer those questions."

As the Colonel uttered those few words "four hundred pounds," he looked straight into Mrs. Jaker's face; and every line in that face, hardened as the woman was by long experience in lying, told him that the shot had gone home. Sir Allan's bank-notes had by some means or other fallen into Jaker's hands.

"I am here as your friend," said the Colonel. "The man you saw last night is a member of the police, and you had nothing to hope for from him. I am here to help you, if I can. A sum of four hundred pounds was stolen from Sir Allan Darnel's house last Tuesday night, and some of that money has been traced to your husband's possession. How did he come by it? Was it he who shot Sir Allan?"

"No, sir, no;" and again Mrs. Jaker called upon the Almighty to witness her truth.

"You have lied to me once already, when you told me Jaker won that money on the racecourse. How can I believe that you are not lying now? A ruffian entered my friend's house at midnight last Tuesday, stole a packet of bank-notes, and shot Sir Allan. The wound is likely to be fatal. Should Sir Allan die before the trial comes on the burglar who shot him will stand charged with his murder. Your husband has had a taste of the law, and he knows that he can't shoot even a rabbit with impunity. He will find it a stiffer business now that he has shot a man."

"He never lifted a hand against Sir Allan.

He hasn't been inside the Park since the time he was falsely accused of stealing one of the deer, three years ago."

"How did he come by that money then?" asked the Colonel, with a severe look.

Almost unconsciously he put on the voice and manner with which he had been wont to address rebellious Sepoys in days gone by. Mrs. Jaker quailed before him.

"He found it," she faltered.

"Found it? Preposterous! People don't find money in hedges. He must have stolen those notes either from the cabinet in Lady Darnel's morning-room; or else he stole them from the person of the man who first stole them. The thing may be a double robbery, but it is a robbery all the same, and you must know your husband to be a thief."

"No, sir." Again Mrs. Jaker called upon the celestial powers. "No, sir, my husband may have been a poacher, but he is not a thief, still less a murderer. Whatever money he had when he went away he came by that money honestly. It was given to him as a free gift."

"That won't do," said the Colonel.

Just at this moment there rang through the old cottage a blood-freezing sound. It was a peal of laughter, long, and loud, and wild, and shrill;

such laughter as no one would expect to hear outside the walls of a lunatic asylum.

"Why you have a maniac on the premises," exclaimed the Colonel. "How is that?" The laughter died away, and then there came a wild snatch of song:

"Grévy à Charenton! Gambetta à Toulon!
Vive le sang! Vive le sang!"

* * * * * *

That was enough for Colonel Stukely. Without waiting for leave from Mrs. Jaker he made for the narrow staircase in a corner of the room, and rushed upstairs as if he had been mounting a breach. There were two rooms above—the door of the first was wide open, Mrs. Jaker's den evidently. The door of the second was shut, and from within came another peal of laughter, almost demoniac in its wild shrillness.

"Otro toro," cried a voice as shrill as the laugh, "Otro toro! Seville, the land of poetry and love, the land of song and dance, of bull fights and beautiful women. Spain—yes—Spain is the place for me."

This time the words were English, spoken as only English lips can speak. Yet, surely, it was a Frenchman who sang that snatch of the Carmagnole just now; and it was a Frenchman of whom Colonel Stukely was in quest.

He opened the door and stood on the threshold, looking into the cottage bedchamber, a fair-sized room under a sloping roof, lighted by a good old dormer window.

The young man whom he had last seen lying amongst the gorse and heather was stretched on a pallet under the window. His head was propped up against the plastered wall, and his eyes were staring straight before him, while his thin hands played with the coverlet. Suddenly, while the Colonel stood watching him, he crouched into a corner of the wall, and flung up his arms above his head like a man recoiling from an enemy.

"The bull!" he shrieked, "the bull is coming at me—keep him off, keep him off. No, it is not the bull. Worse, worse, ten times worse. It is her husband, in his winding sheet, bedabbled with blood. I could never stand blood. Keep him off, keep him off!"

He fell back upon his wretched mattress, his face flushed to crimson, his pupils dilated, the eyeballs rolling restlessly, perspiration rolling in thick beads down his forehead and hollow cheeks. He was a victim to a disease which the Colonel knew only too well, and had seen but too often among Anglo-Indian brandy drinkers, men who had succumbed to the temptations of the climate, and who were sipping brandy and water all day long. He had seen just such paroxysms, and he knew that for the time being they meant raving madness. And this unhappy wretch was Grace Darnel's plighted lover: and if Mr. Penwern came to the cottage by-and-by with his search-warrant he would see this young man and discover the real state of the case—arrest him most likely on suspicion; an arrest which would be followed by an enquiry that might bring Grace's name before the public. How could this wretched creature, maddened by drink, be expected to keep Miss Darnel's secret?

The Colonel looked at his watch. It was a quarter to seven. There was time yet to do something before the detective should appear with his warrant. Mrs. Jaker had followed him upstairs; she was standing at his elbow, watching her strange lodger.

"Come down stairs," said Colonel Stukely, "you can do nothing for that unfortunate wretch. I see you have been giving him brandy," he added, pointing to an empty bottle and a glass on a chair beside the pallet.

"He begged so hard for it that I was obliged to get some for him," answered the woman apologetically.

"How many bottles has he drunk since he has been here? You had better tell me the truth."

"Three—no—I believe it is four," Mrs. Jaker replied meekly.

She was quite overcome by that air of command which was an old habit of the Colonel's.

"That means a bottle a day. I suppose you know that brandy is a deadly poison for a man in his state?"

"No, indeed, sir. It was the only thing that kept him up."

"Don't you think that a doctor would have known better what was good for him? But you dared not send for a doctor."

They had descended the stairs by this time, and the Colonel and Mrs. Jaker were standing face to face in the lower room. The children, not seeing any prospect of a formal breakfast, had possessed themselves of sundry odd crusts and stale slices from a chaotic cupboard, and had gone out into the windy garden to gnaw them, in the company of two or three nomad pigs.

"Now, Mrs. Jaker, let there be no nonsense between you and me," said the Colonel sternly. "I want to save that young man if I can—and in saving him I may be able to save your husband, as in that young man's absence there will be no evidence against Jaker. If the detective comes here with his search-warrant before that young man has been got out of the way, the whole story of how he came here, and how Jaker took that money from him, will come out, and both Jaker and he will be transported for life. A packet of bank-notes stolen from the person is a more serious matter than a snared rabbit, you know, Mrs. Jaker."

Mrs. Jaker did know it. She was trembling in every limb. All that deep-dyed hypocrisy and artfulness by which she had hitherto contrived to hoodwink society deserted her at this crisis of her fate. The Colonel, with his six-feet two, broad shoulders, and soldierly chest, bronzed countenance, and fiercely curving grey moustache, was the most terrible being she had ever looked upon. She stood before him in fear and trembling; and in her agony she told him the unvarnished truth.

"Jaker had been out very late that night—it was the night after the races. He had won a few shillings on True Blue—not ten pounds, sir, no, that was a falsehood—and he stopped drinking at the Coach and Horses till after twelve o'clock—the landlord had to turn 'em out, him and some others. The other men lived in the village, so Jaker had to come home alone. It's a good two mile from the village, and he'd have to pass the park, as you know, sir. There's a right of way in the daytime, but not after the gates are shut."

"Yes, yes, I know."

"But Jaker was never one to stop for gates; so he got over the fence and crossed the park. It would save him a good half-mile. He had got nearly over to the other side—where there's a gate into a narrow lane that leads right on to the Harborough road close against our own lane—when he heard someone groaning. It was so dark that he couldn't tell at first where the groans came from, but when he had groped about a bit he found a man lying under a tree, dying, as he thought. He had a little bottle of spirits in his pocket, that he was bringing home for my rheumatic shoulder, and he forced some of that down the man's throat. It brought him to like, and he asked Jaker if he could find him a shelter for the night, anywheres—he didn't mind how humble—and he could afford to pay for it, as he'd got some money about him, poor as he looked. He had a wild sort of way of talking, Jaker said, and was all of a tremble. Jaker offered to take him to the Coach and Horses, and to knock the landlord up, and get him a bed; but the man would not have that, he wanted to go where nobody would know anything about him. 'Oh,' said my husband, 'I understand.

You're in hiding.' He didn't say yes, nor he didn't say no. So then Jaker offers to take him to our own cottage, and he says, 'Yes, that would do very well, and I can get off by the rail early to-morrow.' So Jaker helps him over the gate, and brings him home—and we makes him up a bed in the room upstairs. But when the bed was made it was hard work to get him to go to it. He sat over the fire, and talked, talked, talked, so fast and so wild like. And he offered my husband a sovereign to go and get a bottle of brandy—and we could hardly make him understand that it was the middle of the night, and that the public-houses were shut. He was dreadfully wild; but Jaker got him up to bed at last, almost carried him, as if he had been a child."

"And when did Jaker find out about the money?" asked the Colonel.

"It was the next day. The young man was in a very low way till he got the brandy. He cried, and said he wished he was dead, and took on dreadfully. But when my husband had fetched a bottle of brandy from the village, and he had drunk the best part of it, he cheered up a little. I made some broth for him in the afternoon, but he would hardly touch it, and he wouldn't take tea, or anything I offered him, except brandy.

He finished the bottle before night, and he was very abusive when my husband refused to get him another. In the evening he went off into a wild state, and raved about something he had under his pillow—a treasure, he called it—and he laughed and said his mother had been very mean to him, but that he had got the best of the bargain."

"His mother," repeated the Colonel, wonderingly. "What could he mean by that?"

And then he reflected that in a paroxysm of *delirium tremens* all a man's words are alike meaningless, and unworthy of consideration.

"While my husband was sitting smoking his pipe beside the bed the young man took the packet out from under his pillow, and Jaker saw that it was a roll of bank notes. The young man counted them over, and talked about the money, and what he was going to do with it, as wild as any madman, and it seemed as if, for half a farthing, he'd have put the notes in the candle, and burnt them all. 'Do you think I care for money for its own sake?' says he. 'Not a bit. I shall drink and game it all away, I daresay, before I'm three months older,' and then Jaker thought what a shame it was that this madman should have all that money to spend in drink and cards, or perhaps to set a light to it when the wild fit was on him—money enough to take us all to Canada, were we'd been pining to go for the last ten years, and to buy us a bit of land, and start us in an honest life—and so, late that night, when the young man had gone off into a restless sleep—he never sleeps above a quarter of an hour at a time—Jaker put his hand softly under the pillow——"

"And stole the notes."

"No, sir. He took out the packet, and looked through the notes, and took half of them, leaving most of the small ones. He took two fifties and five twenties—just enough for our passage money and to buy a little bit of land over there—and he went off early next morning."

"Did he know of any ship sailing for Canada?" asked the Colonel.

"Yes, there was one that was to sail from Plymouth yesterday, and he was in a fever to start by it."

"Plymouth, and yesterday. Mr. Penwern will be a day after the fair," thought the Colonel.

"Did your lodger find out that he had been robbed?" he asked presently.

"Lord, no, sir. He counted the notes over and over again next day in a stupid way, like a man half asleep, and he seemed at first to think that there was something wrong. He missed my husband, too; but when I fetched him his bottle of brandy he was quite content. 'Your husband is dead,' he said. 'I believe I shot him.' Late at night he had a wild fit, and thought the police were after him, and raved and went on dreadful, crying out that he should be hung for murder—just as his father was hung for murder before him. 'No,' he says, 'they didn't hang my father. He was mad, and they locked him up.'"

This fairly startled the Colonel. Why, this was Stuart Mackenzie's story. What could it mean? Could this young man be—— No, the notion was too wild—too horrible. And then it was so idle to attach significance of any kind to the ravings of a maddened drunkard.

In any case there was one thing needful to be done, a thing not easy to be done, and that was to get this young man out of the way before Penwern appeared upon the scene. How was this thing to be accomplished? This man must be conveyed away, and to some safe shelter—but where, and how? Force might be needful to remove him, and a vehicle of some kind. Yet how could the Colonel dare to hire a vehicle in the village where everyone had been put upon the *qui vive* by the bills offering a reward for the apprehension of the robber. Any proceeding at all out of the common was sure to arouse curiosity, and to be talked of all over the village. Secrecy and expedition were alike necessary. The Colonel was fairly nonplussed.

"If we cannot get that young man safely away from this house before eleven o'clock to-day you are likely to spend the night in jail," he said to Mrs. Jaker, turning to her for aid in his desperation.

The poacher's wife was shrewd and crafty, experienced in double dealing. She saw her own danger and she was prompt to face the situation.

"I know of an old barn where he could be comfortable enough for the day," she said. "You could get him away from there after dark."

"Yes, of course, I could do that. I could get a trap from a distance," said the Colonel. "How far is your barn?"

"Ten minutes' walk."

"Good. Then we must try and get him to go there quietly—and of his own accord. I shall look to you to help me. To whom does this barn belong, by the way, and how can you be sure that no one will go there before night?"

"It belongs to Mr. Sommerton, who rents the next farm," answered Mrs. Jaker. "He uses it in summer for some of Squire Colchester's hunters; but it's empty all the winter, and no one goes near it for weeks at a stretch. I don't think there's any fear of anybody going there to-day."

"We must risk it, at any rate," said the Colonel. "You had better stay down here, and be ready to go with me when I bring the young man downstairs."

"I don't think you'll get him to budge," Mrs. Jaker said doubtfully.

But the Colonel had faith in himself. He had been called upon to deal with this species of lunacy before to-day. He had sublime patience, and he knew that if anybody could manage a maniac he could do it.

He went upstairs again. The young man who called himself Camillac was lying in a listless attitude, with his eyes half closed. The Colonel stood in the doorway for some minutes observing him. The face was handsome even in its ruin. Pale, cadaverous, thin and wasted as it was, there were traces of exceptional beauty in the delicately-chiselled features, the perfect proportions of chin, and cheek, and brow, the rich mass of wavy black hair, the silken lashes, and finely-pencilled eyebrows—just the kind of face to catch a schoolgirl's fancy, to dazzle as the countenance of a demi-god. Nor was there any doubt that the man looked like a gentleman. Those slender white hands lying on the patch-work coverlet were hands that had never toiled.

They had shaken a dice box often enough, and handled a billiard cue; but they had never laboured for bread.

Colonel Stukely shut the door sharply, and the sick man started up, looking at him, scared and flurried, and eager.

"Are they there?" he asked.

"Yes," answered the Colonel at a venture, "they have hunted you down. Get up, and put on your boots. I'll get you out of their way if I can."

The young man got up and staggered across the room. He was too weak to move steadily. And then he sank into a broken-down chair, and sat looking about him vaguely. The boots were in a corner—dilapidated, worn-down dress boots. The mud had been roughly wiped off them with a wisp of straw, and that was all. The Colonel picked them up and looked at them before he handed them to their owner. Yes, they would have made just those prints which the detective had shown him on the flower beds. There was the small heel, worn to the quick upon one side, the straight narrow sole, and pointed toe—a French bootmaker's master-piece.

Camillac put on the boots, looking up at the Colonel with a suspicious air as he did so.

"How do I know that you are not one of them," he said.

"Do I look like a policeman?"

"You don't. But that doesn't matter. You may have something to do with them all the same."

"I am Grace Darnel's godfather, and I am here to save you."

"Grace! She sent you then, and she does care for me still. Her letters have been devilish cold for the last six months. I began to think she wanted to throw me over."

"There is no time to talk of that now. If those men get hold of you——"

"Yes, that would be devilish. Are they downstairs? How am I to get away without their seeing me?"

"Mrs. Jaker will keep them talking in the back room while you and I slip out by the front door."

"Where are you going to take me?"

The Colonel explained his plan. He would get a trap at Darnel Park, and pick Camillac up at the barn a little after dusk. It should be a trap that he could drive himself, and he would take the young man to the station, and thence ship him off for London under the charge of his own valet, a man who might be trusted.

What the valet was to do with the young man when he got him to London was a point which the Colonel had not yet had time to consider. But it was a question which must be answered before the evening.

Camillac was not easily managed. At one

moment he was white with terror at the thought of those men below, believing in them firmly: and in the next moment he doubted their existence, and was afraid of the Colonel. He knelt down by the pallet presently, and took the packet of notes from under his pillow, and thrust it inside his ragged shirt. He did this in a secret way, glancing furtively at the Colonel all the time.

"How do I know that you don't mean to rob me?" he muttered. "I have missed some money already in this house. I believe it is a den of thieves."

"If you suspect *me* I had better wish you good morning," said the Colonel.

This threw the wretch into a panic of fear and self-abasement. He flung his arms round the Colonel's neck; he entreated him to keep off those devils, who wanted to drag him away and hang him.

"I didn't mean to kill him," he said. "I shot him without thinking. The pistol was there, don't you know, ready to my hand, as if Satan himself had put it in my way. Save me, save me—hide me. I am not a murderer!"

"Be quick, then," said the Colonel decisively, "there is no time for fooling. If you want to escape those men you must not lose an instant."

He went downstairs, and Camillac followed him like a beaten hound.

"You've got the policeman out of the way," said the Colonel, winking at Mrs. Jaker. "That was clever of you. And now come and show us the way to this barn."

He put the young man's arm through his, and led him out into the garden. Camillac was in a pitiable state of weakness, and could not have gone three steps without help. But the fresh morning air revived him a little, and he was able to get over the ground, supported and aided by the Colonel. The barn was in sight, across a couple of fields. They skirted these open fields, keeping close to the hedgerows, where there was a hard, well-beaten track, and where their feet would leave no perceptible traces. The barn was never locked. It was a large airy building—old, but substantially built, with great heavy rafters, and patches of open sky showing here and there through the great dark roof.

"Why this is Noah's ark," cried Camillac. "What a rotten old hulk. We shall be wrecked in the first storm."

There was some straw in a corner. Camillac flung himself down upon it. The Colonel took off his heavy ulster and spread it over the shivering wretch.

"Get through the day quietly here, sleep if you can; and I'll come to fetch you at dusk," said the Colonel.

"I can't get on without brandy," answered the other. "You can bring me a bottle," he said to Mrs. Jaker, handing her a sovereign from his waistcoat pocket.

The young man's possession of this gold puzzled the Colonel, but he concluded that the Jakers had changed one of his notes for him, albeit Mrs. Jaker had not mentioned that fact in her confession just now.

"She shall take care of you," said the Colonel; "but remember you are in constant peril of being arrested as long as you remain in the neighbourhood of Darnel Park. So you had better keep as quiet as you possibly can till I come to fetch you." And with this injunction Colonel Stukely left him.

There was no lock to the barn-door, but the Colonel found a primitive and ingenious way of fastening it outside by means of a bit of wood and a strip of iron, which he twisted under and over the latch, so as to render it a difficult matter for Mr. Camillac to get out. As they went back to the lane the Colonel gave Mrs. Jaker her instructions.

"You are to take him no raw brandy," he said, "unless you want to hasten his death. You must get a couple of pounds of beef and make some beef tea—as strong as you can make it. You can put half a wine-glass of brandy in a breakfast-cup of beef tea, and try to make him drink that. He is in a terribly low state, and will die from exhaustion unless he takes some kind of nourishment."

The Colonel could not help thinking within himself that it would be a very good thing for Grace, and everybody else, if this young adventurer were to die; but as an honest, God-fearing man, Weldon Stukely knew that it was his duty to try and save him. He walked home quickly, not much the worse for the sacrifice of his ulster, though it was a sharp October morning. He entered the hall with the air of a man who had been for a stroll in the gardens, just as the eight-day clock was striking nine.

No gong sounded for meals in this time of trouble. All noises in the house were hushed, save the musical chime of the clocks.

Dora Darnel was coming downstairs with her key-basket on her arm, like a jailer.

"What is the last report?" asked the Colonel, when he had wished her good morning.

"The night-nurse says there is an improvement, but I am always afraid to trust these people," added Dora, as if all hirelings were vipers. "However, Mr. Friedricson is to be here to-day, and we shall get the truth from him."

"Has Penwern started on his mission yet?" asked the Colonel, trying to seem careless.

"He went out at eight this morning."

"Good," thought the Colonel, "it must be ten before he can be at Mrs. Jaker's with this warrant."

The famous London surgeon was to be at Darnel at eleven that day, and was to extract the bullet, if he saw his way to performing that operation safely. Lady Darnel knew that this day was to be the crisis in her husband's fate. Before the day was over she would know, perhaps, whether he was to be spared or lost to her; whether joy or despair was to be her portion. She waited the issue in a silent agony. She would not leave her room except to creep into the corridor and crouch listening on the ground outside her husband's door. She would see no one except nurses and doctor.

The nurse's favourable account of last night was the first gleam of hope.

"You think he will get better now," she said, clasping the woman's hand. "You believe that we shall save him?"

"I couldn't undertake to say so much as that, my lady, but Sir Allan certainly had a much quieter night," the woman answered calmly.

When Mr. Friedricson and the local doctor came upstairs they found Lady Darnel standing in the corridor, neatly dressed in her gray cloth gown and linen collar, beautiful, calm as a statue; but there was a strained look about her eyes and forehead, a restlessness in the muscles of the mouth which told the great surgeon how her nerves were racked.

The two medical men were closeted in the sick room for more than an hour, Lady Darnel, and Grace, and Dora waiting in the corridor all the time. They stood in a little group at the further end of the corridor, not daring to be near the sick room lest they should be in the way at some critical moment. Both the nurses were in attendance, everything had been prepared for the operation. There was no rushing in and out, there were no sudden unforeseen requirements, there was no confusion. There was only intense and agonising anxiety for those who watched and listened without.

At last the door opened. Lady Darnel rushed towards it, white as death. She met the famous surgeon, a man of tall, commanding figure, a man who looked a tower of strength in the hour of calamity. Her lips moved as she looked up at him appealingly, but no sound came from them.

"Do not agitate yourself, my dear Lady Darnel," said the kindly voice of the operator, "everything has gone most favourably. We have extracted the bullet. There is every reason for hopefulness."

"Praise be to God," she cried fervently. "May I go to my husband? May I stay with him, and help them to nurse him?"

"Not yet, Lady Darnel. It is more than ever necessary that he should be kept quiet."

"But I am pining to see him. It has been such a weary time. I should be so quiet. I believe he would be happier if I were there. Has he not asked for me?"

"He is hardly conscious at present. The fever is much abated, the delirium much milder, but he is not in his right senses yet. When he is he will be sure to ask for you."

"Unless he is strangely changed," said Clare, with a touch of bitterness.

She knew not what trouble might wait for her in the future, even when her dear one was snatched from the jaws of death.

"He must be kept very quiet, he must see no one except his nurses for the next few days. We have every reason to believe that all will go well."

"Every reason," murmured the local authority.

"But in such a critical case there is no such thing as certainty. The uttermost care will be required," said Mr. Friedricson.

This was all. But, oh, how much it was to be able to hope.

After breakfast the Colonel had an interview with his valet; and between them they made out a plan for the disposal of Victor de Camillac. The valet had an old mother—he spoke of her as an accident in his life—who lived in a pretty little street off Islington Green, and who let lodgings to single gentlemen. There had been a dearth of single gentlemen lately; or rather the supply had all been absorbed by the musical families, who had tennis lawns and bath rooms, and agreeable daughters, and who eked out Somerset House incomes by partial-boarding single gentlemen; so that the valet's old mother had to bemoan the emptiness of her rooms.

"She cooks for them and does for them better than they can be done by in your shabby genteel musical families," said the valet; "but they're all alike, taken by a bit of show—a few flowers and fal-lals about a room, and a young lady to play the piano to them."

It was settled that Nicolls, the valet, should take Camillac to his mother's house, hire a nurse for him, call in a doctor, and put him in a fair way of recovery.

The Colonel had his own ideas about getting the young man out of England so soon as he should be well enough to be put on board ship; but there was no occasion to discuss these ideas with Nicolls.

CHAPTER XI.

"LOVE, SEE THY LOVER HUMBLED AT THY FEET."

THE luncheon at Darnel Park that day was more cheerful than it had been since the catastrophe of nearly a week ago. For the first time since that awful night the household had been bidden to hope, and hope filled the hearts of all, high and low. The countenance of old Purdew, the butler, beamed with gladness as he poured out Colonel Stukely's glass of Manzanilla, and gave his sweeping professional glance round the luncheon-table to see that all things were correct, before he retired to his own substantial meal in the housekeeper's room. Even Miss Darnel was amiable; and poor Grace was radiant, despite those secret griefs which gnawed her heart.

"I can bear anything," she said to herself, "if my father recovers."

She was dying for another talk with the Colonel. She wanted to hear what news the detective had brought last night, and if any fresh circumstances had been brought to light bearing upon that horrible suspicion about Victor de Camillac. There had been as yet no opportunity for any confidential talk with her friend. He had been in his own room all the morning, and just as luncheon was over, and she was hoping to get a little walk on the terrace with her godfather, the butler announced Mr. Colchester, and at this announcement Grace flew upstairs to her sanctum with as scared an aspect as if the man had said that smallpox or scarlet fever was in the drawing-room.

Dora, always ready to do the honours of her

brother's house, sailed off to receive the Lord of the Manor; while the Colonel went to the stables to give an order for the dog-cart. He would drive himself, he told the chief coachman, taking only Nicolls with him. The cart was to be ready for him at a quarter to six. He was going to Scadleigh station to meet a friend who would arrive by the seven o'clock train. The Colonel's position as Sir Allan's oldest friend gave him a wide authority in the stables, and nobody presumed to question his orders.

"You'd better take Dandy, sir," said the coachman. "He's a good goer, and he don't mind trains."

Dora found Mr. Colchester in very low spirits. He was cheered by the good news about Sir Allan; but even that could not remove the cloud of gloom which hung around him as a garment.

"People are so d—— ill-natured! I beg your pardon, Miss Darnel, only I have really no patience. They have been saying such things about this business, making a mystery of it, insinuating that it has something to do with Lady Darnel's past history."

"Indeed," said Dora eagerly.

She had seen a few of her own particular friends since the catastrophe, spinsters of her own standing, or elderly young ladies strong in tennis and piety, and to these she had unfolded her doubts, vaguely, mysteriously, alleging no evil, but hinting at a good deal. And now the bread she had scattered upon the waters was coming back to her tenfold. She was not deliberately malicious, she did not even know, in the depths of her own conscience, that she was acting cruelly and unfairly to Lady Darnel. She fancied herself a model of truth, justice, magnanimity. She told herself that in all things she was loyal and devoted to her brother. When she saw him cheated and imposed upon it was her duty to defend him, to watch for him, to the eyes and ears for him whom a wild infatuation had made blind and deaf.

"A parcel of tabbies," exclaimed the young Squire, unconscious that he was alluding to Dora's chosen friends, the select and superior elements in county society, the handful of corn amidst the chaff. "I dropped in at Scoville's yesterday" (Major Scoville was a mighty hunter), "and there were a pack of women at tea, and they all set on to gabble about Sir Allan's danger; he was going to die, they were all cock-sure of that, a set of ghouls; and then they began to wonder and to speculate. How odd it all was, they had never liked Lady Darnel. They admitted that she was handsome, or had been handsome; but they had never been able to bring themselves to believe in her, though they had tried to do so, for Sir Allan's sake. As if Sir Allan could care a hang what they believed."

"He has cared," said Dora solemnly, "all men are sensitive, on these points. Why in France half the duels one reads about are fought for no stronger reason. I told you the other day that my brother has suffered acutely from the consequences of his most unhappy marriage. Was there anything more said?"

"A great deal. They began to talk about some man—a young man—dressed no better than a tramp, but very good-looking, and with the air of a broken-down gentleman, who was seen near Darnel Park late in the afternoon before the night on which Sir Allan was shot. It seems that Miss Mowbray and her sister Jane—you know Jane."

"As well as if she were my own sister. She is one of the most truthful girls I know."

"I shouldn't call her a girl," said Edward bluntly; "anyhow she is quite old enough to know what she's talking about. She and Miss Mowbray had been out to tea. It is their normal condition, don't you know, to be drinking tea in somebody's house every afternoon; and they were going home in the dusk, and they were a little frightened, timid young flutterers; so that when a young man jumped up from the bank, where he had been lying, they were ready to drop. They expected to be robbed of their watches at the least; but he only asked them the way to Darnel Park. He spoke like a gentleman, and he looked like a gentleman, in spite of his shabby clothes. He was not dressed any better than a tramp, they say."

"That may have been a disguise," said Dora suspiciously.

"Precisely! The same idea occurred to me," said Mr. Colchester, also suspicious. That candid nature of his was getting perverted by jealousy. He was puzzled by the inconsistency of Grace's conduct. She had almost admitted that she loved him and then had declared that she would never be his wife. There must be some reason for such a contradiction; and this shabby, good-looking young man lurking mysteriously in the neighbourhood of Darnel Park might be the reason.

"Did the Mowbrays see any more of this person?" asked Dora.

"He followed them a little way, and questioned them curiously about Darnel Park. Were the family at home, Sir Allan, Lady Darnel, Miss Darnel. He seemed to know all about them, had their names quite pat. The Mowbrays answered him civilly, out of sheer funk. They thought he was a genteel beggar, who might change his mind any moment and go for their watches. They hurried home as fast as they could directly they got clear of him. Now this fact, taken in conjunction with the night attack upon Sir Allan, is certainly rather startling."

"It is more than startling," exclaimed Dora. "I have felt convinced from the very first that it was no common robber who entered the house that night."

And then she spoke of the footsteps which she had heard on the terrace between ten and eleven—the slow stealthy tread, like that of a man pacing up and down, waiting and watching for his opportunity. No doubt that was the footfall of this very man.

"Who could he be, do you think?" asked Edward.

"Some one connected with Lady Darnel's past life," answered Dora decisively.

"Some secret lover of Grace's," thought Edward.

"His shabby clothes were only a disguise, you may depend," said Dora.

"But the fact that the money was taken seems to point to a burglar," added Edward dubiously.

"The money may have been taken only as a blind—not taken at all, perhaps, only hidden somewhere about the room where it will be found later on. The man was a gentleman, he went to that room to see Lady Darnel, and on finding himself surprised by my poor brother he shot him in order to escape recognition. Who knows what hatred and jealousy he may have felt against poor

Allan, if he was, as I fear, a cast-off sweetheart of Lady Darnel's—jilted, perhaps, in order that she might marry my deluded brother."

Dora Darnel put her little story together so neatly, had such a glib assured air in the telling of it, that Edward Colchester was almost inclined to believe her. And yet there were difficulties.

"This person was described as a young man," he said, "and Lady Darnel is not a young woman. A former admirer of hers would hardly be a youth."

"Those Mowbray girls were too frightened to be very good judges as to a stranger's age, and again some women have such perverse ideas. To my mind Lady Darnel is just the kind of person to have encouraged a young admirer, and then to have thrown him over directly she saw a chance of a good establishment."

"You have not a high opinion of Lady Darnel," said Mr. Colchester, shocked at the undisguised venom of her tone.

"Has the county a high opinion of her? Have you a high opinion of her?" asked Dora contemptuously.

"I have always liked her immensely; but of course, I would rather think ill of her than of Grace."

"Of Grace," screamed Miss Darnel, "what has Grace to do with it? Surely you cannot suppose this man to be an admirer of my niece."

She pronounced the possessive pronoun as if the mere fact of relationship to her made wrong-doing of any kind impossible.

"I—I—have been inclined to fear that he might have come here to see Grace," faltered the Squire, blushing vehemently.

"To see Grace! Impossible! It was in Lady Darnel's room that he was found. All Lady Darnel's conduct since that dreadful night has indicated a mystery. Never was guilt more plainly expressed than by that wretched woman's words and manner. Why she started up in her sleep the next morning, screaming out that it was her fault, it was she who had murdered her husband. And that idiotic detective from London has chosen to start upon an entirely false scent. He has taken it into his head that Jaker stole the money; just because Jaker happened to change a twenty pound note in the village two days ago."

"Did he!" exclaimed Edward. "That looks queer. Jaker is bad enough for anything."

"But Jaker would have no motive for breaking into Lady Darnel's morning-room. He could not know that the money was there. There was nothing to take him to that particular room."

"Nothing, except the fact that it is the most accessible room in the house," said Edward. "I should like to see Grace, if she would let me. She will not be quite so unhappy now that Sir

Allan is in a more hopeful condition. Ah, there she is in the garden. I'll go out to her. If I asked to see her I daresay she would say no."

He took a hurried adieu, and was off to the garden before Miss Darnel could say another word. He had caught sight of a tall, slim figure in the distance, soft brown hair blown by the autumn wind. Grace was walking up and down by the shrubbery, just where she had told him that his case was hopeless. She had flown up to her room to avoid him, as if he were a pestilence; and yet here she was walking where he could hardly fail to see her as he left the house. It was just one of those inconsistent things which young ladies of Grace Darnel's age are prone to do. Edward Colchester ran across the lawn and joined her. He ran his fastest, half afraid that she would vanish amidst the wilderness of shrubs before he could reach her. But she did not even try to avoid him. She gave him her hand frankly, and he took it, but with a certain coldness which startled her. His bosom was rent by horrible suspicions about that stranger, whom the Mowbrays had described to him. Till those doubts should be satisfied, the master-passion jealousy took the place of the master-passion love. He made some common-place remark about the improvement in her father's health, and then began abruptly to talk of the stranger who had met the

Mowbrays. Grace's sudden look of fear at his very first allusion to this man told him that the man was no stranger to her. His doubts were too well founded. The man had come to Darnel to see Grace. He must needs be some disreputable suitor whose acquaintance she had formed away from home, and who came by stealth to prosecute his suit, or to complete his conquest.

"Your aunt thinks that this man came to see Lady Darnel," he said.

"To see Lady Darnel. How wicked, how unjust! So like my aunt," cried Grace indignantly.

"For what other purpose could he have come —except as a thief?"

"He is not a thief," said Grace, beginning with a rush, as if about to say a great deal, and then becoming suddenly silent.

For a moment she had been inclined to say, "He came to see me." She had been tempted to tell Edward Colchester the story of her entanglement, the dishonouring chain which she had forged for herself. Yet, why should she so lower herself in his eyes? She had refused to be his wife. Surely that was enough. She had sacrificed her own happiness in order to be true to that fatal promise. It was not for her to apologise to a rejected lover for her folly. To him she owed no allegiance.

"He is not a thief," echoed Edward. "How

prompt you are to defend him. You know this person then?"

"I am not going to be catechised by you," she retorted angrily.

"I would not presume to catechise. Only you must admit that under certain circumstances a man has a right to be curious. Your father, my father's dearest friend, a man I honour and love, has been nearly murdered. I am told of a young man who has been seen lurking about the park —in all probability the criminal—and when I mention the fact you take up the cudgels in this man's defence. What can I think, Grace; except that there is a mystery here in which you are in some way concerned."

"You can think what you please," she answered coldly. "I do not consider myself accountable to you for my conduct. And now I must wish you good afternoon. I am going indoors to hear the latest news of my father."

A quarter of an hour ago she was longing to see him—she had purposely put herself in the way of seeing him; and now she left him in anger, left him tortured by jealousy.

In the hall Grace met Purdew, the butler, and from him she learnt that Colonel Stukely had gone out walking. This was a blow, as she was dying for a talk with her friend and counsellor.

Lacking this comfort she shut herself in her own room, restless, unhappy, and full of fear.

The day wore on. Lady Darnel spent the afternoon in prayer and thanksgiving. Each new report from the sick-room was more cheering than the last. Sir Allan was sleeping peacefully—the weary brain so long tormented by the wild visions of fever was now at rest. The tide had turned. Soon, very soon, Clare Darnel might hope to take her place beside the sick-bed, to see the beloved face smile a fond welcome to the loving wife.

Grace was on the watch all that afternoon for Colonel Stukely's return; but to her surprise she saw him driving away from the house at a few minutes before six, his valet sitting at the back of the cart. This seemed a very mysterious proceeding. The dogcart had not been brought to the hall door. The Colonel had got into it in the stable yard, and drove rapidly round to the avenue and away, like a man who did not wish his departure to be observed. Grace spent an hour and a half of supreme anxiety, and at half-past seven a little pencilled note was brought her, in her godfather's well-known hand.

"I am obliged to go to London, dear Gracie, in your interests. Don't be anxious. All will be well. It may be some days—perhaps more than a week—before I can go back to Darnel. Your scampish friend is alive, but in a very sad condition. I shall do all I can for him, and I shall not lose sight of him till I have obtained your release. So you may consider yourself free to be kind to poor Colchester. The man is not a Frenchman. You have, therefore, been grossly deceived by him, and that fact alone should cancel any promise you may have given him. Ever your faithful friend, W. S."

"Not a Frenchman," thought Grace indignantly. "What an impostor! And he spoke French so beautifully, and wrote such lovely letters. I daresay they are full of faults in grammar which my ignorance could not detect."

The Colonel said not a word as to whether Camillac was or was not implicated in the crime at Darnel. It was cruel of him to leave her unenlightened, Grace thought.

The dogcart had been driven back to Darnel by a man from the station hotel, at Scadleigh. The Colonel sent a second little note to Dora, apologising for his abrupt departure, and asking her to telegraph a daily bulletin to him at the club where he would breakfast every morning. He had a *pied à terre* in the shape of a second floor in the neighbourhood of St. James's Street.

Three days had gone by since the Colonel's departure, and the progress of the invalid had been satisfactory throughout that time. Pulse and temperature had gradually fallen almost to a normal condition, the wound was going on favourably, the patient had tranquil nights, and was able to take a little more nourishment than at the beginning of his illness. And thus there came an hour when the family doctor felt that he could no longer forbid the presence of wife and kindred in the sick-room.

"We must do nothing rash," he said to Clare, in the presence of Grace and Dora. "You may spend an hour or so with Sir Allan to-day, Lady Darnel; and to-morrow, if all go well, Miss Darnel and Miss Grace might see him. But it had better be one at a time."

"It is very odd if I cannot see my brother as soon as he is fit to see anyone," observed Dora, pallid with anger, yet speaking with her accustomed suavity. "We have been companions for a great many years. I have never had a secret from him, or he from me."

"That fact, interesting as it is, would not make your presence less agitating, my dear Miss Darnel," said the doctor. "Lady Darnel has the first claim—a wife's claims are paramount, you know—and you and Miss Grace must wait for to-morrow. And now, Lady Darnel, remember what I have told you about our patient. Not one agitating word—no show of emotion on your part. He is too weak to bear anything of that kind."

"I will be careful," said Clare, clasping his hand. She was very pale, her lips quivering with nervous excitement, and yet joy beamed in her eyes. The moment so ardently longed for had come at last. The bolted door by which she had watched and listened was no longer to be an impassable barrier between her and her beloved.

"You can go to him now," said the doctor, "but remember you are to stay only an hour—one hour by the clock. It is just twelve. You will leave him at one."

"And is that to be *all?* Am I not to see him again all day?"

"I shall be here in the evening, and if I find there has been no mischief done—if Sir Allan is quite calm and comfortable, I may—well, I will be very indulgent and let you see him again for ten minutes."

"I will be obedient," said Lady Darnel, opening the door as she spoke.

She went softly into the room—the spacious, old-fashioned bed chamber, which looked larger in the semi-darkness of half-drawn window curtains and lowered blinds. It was a noble room, furnished with the artistic cabinet-work of the Jacobean era — old walnutwood wardrobes and secretaires, old cherrywood chairs with elaborately carved backs. The only modern piece of furniture was the low, broad brass bedstead, without a vestige of drapery. The wide, deep hearth, with its old blue and white tiles, and basket grate, and high mantelpiece, was a study for a painter of still-life. The window curtains were of old brocade, red and tawny. The room had a look of sombre old-world luxury, very pleasant to the eye.

The nurse rose, and slipped very quietly away to the adjoining dressing-room as Lady Darnel approached the bed. Sir Allan was lying with the firelight shining on his face. Oh, what a changed countenance—shrunken, pallid, as with the lines of death. For the first time Clare understood how near he had been to death. It was almost as if she were looking upon a face she had never seen before. The eyes—those dear eyes that used to gaze upon her with such love—looked at her now with a strange, dim, far-away expression.

Shocked, horrified, by the extent of the change, so much greater than she had expected, Clare Darnel sank into a chair by the bedside, waiting, hoping for some little word of greeting from those pale lips; but no such word came. Her husband lifted his eyes to her face and looked at her gravely, mournfully. His wasted, half-transparent hand lay on the silken coverlet. She bent and kissed it; but he drew it away the next moment with a quick, nervous gesture, as if the touch of her lips offended him.

She set a watch upon herself, remembering the doctor's injunctions.

"My beloved," she murmured softly. "It is such a happiness to me to see you once again—to be allowed to sit by your bedside for a little while."

There were tears in her voice. The shock of his altered appearance—his strange manner—were alike agitating to her; and she had to be so careful lest her agitation should communicate itself to him. She waited, with her heart beating vehemently—waited for some word of loving welcome. In vain.

"You are much better, Allan, Mr. Danvers tells me. You will soon be among us again."

"Mr. Danvers is vastly hopeful."

How weak and faint his voice sounded; how strangely cold his tone.

"The house is so dreary without you," she said tremulously, trying to command herself, not for an instant forgetting the doctor's warning. "I have not been downstairs since—that awful night."

"Do you think it was necessary to carry on the comedy so long?" he said, with a scathing sneer. "But I forgot, you are such a skilful actress that the deception would cost you no effort. You, who have deceived me so long, would find no difficulty in hoodwinking the outside world."

"Allan," she exclaimed breathlessly.

Was this delirium? His words were measured, deliberate, cool as the speech of a judge who calmly discusses the details of crime and wrong-doing. She could not believe that his mind was wandering. The doctor had told her that fever and delirium were past. The patient's extreme weakness was now the only peril; and that weakness made any emotion dangerous. If some dark cloud of suspicion had obscured her husband's mind—if love had been changed into loathing, she dared not question him, she dared not strive to set herself right. She must wait, and suffer in patience.

Silently, prayerfully, Clare Darnel sat by her husband's sick-bed, and listened to the ticking of the clock, to the falling of the wood ashes from the old basket grate. She could pray for her beloved; yes, that was all she could do in this hour of severance—severance, albeit she was sitting by his side. She could pray, and put her trust in God. She could not believe that any estrangement between herself and her husband could last. Life had been made very bitter to her in the days of her first marriage—a long period of pain and anxiety, growing from bad to worse, till it culminated in the tragedy at Mallow Barracks. And there had followed further trouble about her son. And then, after she had done with hope, after she had told herself that joy and gladness were not for her, there had come the awakening of a new love, the beginning of a new life, days of exceeding sweetness. Was that bright time all over now, she wondered, and was she to go back into the darkness, and pain, and desolation. No, she could not believe that fate would be so cruel, that she was to be ever the victim of other people's sins—the scape-goat to suffer for the folly and crime of her belongings. No, all would be well again between herself and her beloved when once she could talk to him freely. He would not revenge upon her the wrong-doing of her son, although it had gone near to cost him his life. She knew Allan Darnel's generous heart too well to believe that. But for the time being there was a gulf which she dared not attempt to cross. Whatever he might suspect, whatever evil he might think of her she could not set herself right yet awhile.

So she sat with folded hands, meekly, quiet as the figure of a saint in a cathedral niche, praying for him whose thoughts had wronged her, praying for the restoration of the confidence and the bliss of old, when he and she had been in all things of one mind. And so the moments stole gently by till the hour was done, and as the clock struck she rose to leave the room.

"I must go now, Allan," she said softly. "Mr. Danvers only allowed me one hour. Can I get you anything, or do anything for you before I go? It would be such a pleasure to me to do you some small service."

"Thanks, you are very kind. No, there is nothing."

He spoke courteously, but as coldly as if he were addressing a stranger.

"*Au revoir*, Allan. I may come again to look at you in the evening, perhaps."

He did not forbid her to return. He let her depart in silence.

He looked after her with sad, reproachful eyes till she was gone, and then turned his head upon the pillow and groaned aloud. Yes, he loved her still. She was as dear to him as she had ever been: she whom he believed to be the falsest and vilest among women: she who had admitted a lover beneath her husband's roof at midnight—a desperado who, seeing his mistress's good name at stake, had tried to murder the husband in order to save the wife.

Yes, he recalled in this bitter hour, as he had recalled again and again since the awakening from the long agony of delirium, he recalled once again the memory of that hideous night. He remembered how in his sleep, the heavy sleep of fatigue, he had vaguely heard the murmur of two voices in the adjoining room, his wife's voice and another; how, even in sleep, he had wondered at those voices, wondered that his wife should be talking; how, struggling half-consciously to arouse himself, he had at last awakened to hear his wife speaking and a man's voice replying. Then came silence and the sudden shutting of a door. He had risen hurriedly, put on his dressing jacket, and opened the door of the morning-room. On the very threshold he stopped, seeing a man standing by the table—a man whose dark handsome face impressed itself upon him in that one instant.

He could recall those dark, flashing eyes, the hectic flush upon hollow cheeks, the haughty carriage of the head; but he could remember no more. He could not have told the man's age, or the clothes he wore. The figure stood before him for a moment only, dark, tall, defiant; then there was a flash, and all was dark.

The face had haunted him in his delirium—the figure, with pistol pointed at him, had pursued him through the dark mazes of fever—and now while he lay weak as a child, helpless, hopeless, broken-hearted, the dark evil face was with him still, a haunting presence.

And he believed that his wife was false to him, an arch deceiver from the very beginning of their acquaintance. He believed that she had put aside some dearer love for the sake of the position he was able to offer, and that all her subsequent life with him had been one elaborate comedy, so perfect in its dissimulation that he had lived in a fool's paradise, deeming himself the happiest of men. Then came the preparations for the Italian tour. The lover had heard of this intended journey, had grown desperate, perhaps, at the idea of a prolonged separation, and had insisted on an interview. Urged by an angry man, irrevocably lost by her conduct in the past, Clare Darnel had not stopped short at this last infamy. She had admitted her lover at midnight, beneath her husband's roof. And she came to him to-day in her calm, pale beauty, looking at him with her eyes softened by unshed tears; she kissed him with her false lips; she acted her part of shameless hypocrisy to the last, and did not shrink from the man whose heart she had broken, whose life had well nigh been sacrificed to her infamy.

"If I had died from that wound she would have married her old lover—married him with his hand red with my blood—married as Mary married Bothwell," he thought, "and the settlement which my doating folly secured to her would have made their future days easy. And this is the woman I have trusted—this is the woman whom I gave as a mother to my innocent child."

The doctor came in the evening, and was not altogether satisfied with his patient's appearance.

"You look worried," he said. "I thought Lady Darnel's visit would have cheered you. I expected to see a marked improvement. How has he taken his nourishment, nurse?"

"Not over-well, sir," answered a prim little person in grey. "Sir Allan sent away the partridge scarcely touched, and he only took a spoonful of his custard."

"No use trying to pamper you with dainties," said the doctor facetiously. "We shall have to put you back upon Brand's essence if you don't take care. Sir Allan must take a plate of invalid turtle for his supper, nurse, and you must give him a glass of dry sherry after it."

Sir Allan looked supremely indifferent to the supper question.

"If Lady Darnel has any idea of coming to see me this evening, you might tell her that she had better not. I do not think I am strong enough to see people yet," he said presently, while the doctor was feeling his pulse, watch in hand.

"I don't think you are. You have quite disappointed me," replied Mr. Danvers.

Clare was waiting in the corridor when the doctor went out.

"May I see him again to-night?" she asked eagerly.

"Not to-night. He is very low—out of spirits—altogether depressed, a natural reaction after that violent fever. He must be left to himself for a few days more."

"And I am not to see him again—for a few days?" exclaimed Clare dejectedly.

"Come, dear Lady Darnel, I have let you have an hour with him. I have been very indulgent; too indulgent, I fear, for the result has not been favourable. In Sir Allan's extreme weakness any excitement is bad. The thread has been strained to its thinnest point—an extra strain might snap it!"

"I will not go near him for a week," said Clare, bursting into tears. "He was not himself to-day. If you had not told me that the delirium was over——"

"Oh, his mind is clear enough. That is all right."

"*Is* it? Are you sure that he is in his right senses?"

"As sure as I can be of everything. He is perfectly calm and reasonable this evening. There is no fever. There is weakness, and there is a profound depression. We can only hope for the return of strength. His spirits will revive as he gets stronger. Good-night, Lady Darnel."

"Good-night," she answered despondently going back to her room.

She still kept herself secluded from the rest of the family. She could not bring herself to return to the common routine of daily life, its irksome forms and ceremonies, the hollow semblance of peace where there was no peace. In the seclusion of her own apartments she could abandon herself freely to the fever of her soul, could start up from her seat and walk up and down the room, could dull the agony of her heart by quick movement, by restless wandering in and out from the room to the corridor.

"Can he doubt me—or does he guess the truth? Does he suspect that it was my son, my reprobate son who has just missed being his murderer? If he did he is too generous to blame me for my son's guilt, to accuse me of hypocrisy. Hypocrite, how and why?" she asked herself piteously.

And then she remembered how, in telling Allan Darnel the history of her unhappy son, she had spoken of him as of one whom she believed to be dead. The knowledge that he still lived had come to her very soon after her marriage and she had kept that knowledge from her husband. That had been her greatest sin. In her agony as a mother, ashamed of the son who only appealed to her for money, whose vices and follies had been a continual drain upon her purse, she had shrunk from the acknowledgment of his existence. She had hoped always to keep him at arm's length, till at last repentance and reform should come, and he should begin a new life in a new land. The new land had been tried, and had proved a failure as a means of reform; but he was young enough for the possibility of reformation, and the mother's heart still clung to that hope.

In this and in this only had she acted as a hypocrite. She had kept the knowledge of this burden to herself. She had kept the secret of this ever-present care. This perpetual dread of what the day might bring forth, this constant anxiety had preyed upon her, undermining her health, making her fitful and low-spirited; and her anxious husband had told himself that it was her womanly pride that suffered, that it was the coldness of his old friends which made her unhappy.

"I will tell him all, by-and-by, when he is strong enough to bear an agitating conversation," she said to herself, after long meditation upon her husband's conduct, "and if I find that I have lost his love—well, I must bear the blow. It will not be the first of my trials, and it ought to be the last. If that loss do not kill me nothing can."

Second only to the horror of having forfeited her husband's love was the agonising thought of her son's infamy. A thief, and only by God's mercy a little short of a murderer. He, her only son, had fired upon her husband with the intent to kill him. He had escaped from that house, carrying with him four hundred pounds of stolen money. Where was he now? A felon, a marked man, pursued by detectives; perhaps before long to stand in the felon's dock, and to answer for his crime. Then the whole story of his wretched existence, of his mother's bitter burden, would be unfolded for the gratification of the curious; and all those old friends of Sir Allan's who had held themselves aloof from his second wife would say, "We did well to suspect this woman's antecedents. The mother of such a son could not be a good woman."

Not once in her conversation with Grace had Lady Darnel hinted at her knowledge of the girl's acquaintance with the adventurer who had called himself Victor de Camillac. To do that would have been to reveal too much. She was determined to guard her step-daughter from any future dealings with her son, should he ever again dare to present himself upon the scene. But it was her desire, if possible, to get him out of the country before he was called upon to pay the forfeit of his crime. Miss Darnel's promptitude in putting the case into the hands of the police made her position all the more difficult. Her only hope was that Mr. Penwern, having got upon a false scent, would continue to go astray, and would devote himself to the pursuit of Jaker, while the real criminal was making his escape. It was not to Dora Darnel that Clare owed her knowledge of Mr. Penwern's movements. That lady went about with locked lips, the very incarnation of secrecy. But in a country house secrets of this kind pervade the air. Mr. Penwern had been made very comfortable in the housekeeper's room; and though he had been discreet he had not altogether been silent. Lady Darnel's maid told her that Jaker was known to have stolen the money; and that Mr. Penwern wanted to stop him from getting off to America. The idea of his guilt had been confirmed by the disappearance of Mrs. Jaker, whose cottage had been found empty one morning, she and her brood of brats having slipped away under cover of the darkness, almost as quietly as Robin Goodfellow and his goblin crew.

CHAPTER XII.

"THEN BE WE, EACH AND ALL, FORGIVEN."

A WEEK went by, a week of misery for every one at Darnel Park, and for at least one person outside the gates; a week which had brought no new tidings of any kind. Mr. Penwern had gone back to Scotland Yard a confessed failure; and Dora was scathing in her contempt for the detective force. He had eaten and drunk; he had been handsomely paid for his services; he had gone upon expensive journeys to Liverpool, and Plymouth, and Cork; but he had failed to arrest the footsteps of Jaker or even to discover what white wings had wafted Jaker and his fortunes westward. Among the crowd of emigrants for that Western Paradise, the poacher, a marked man in the neighbourhood of Darnel, had been but an insignificant unit; and he had left no trace behind him in the memory of dock labourers or quayside loiterers.

The note changed by Jaker at the village shop had been identified by Sir Allan's bankers as one of the notes issued to him. This fact established Jaker's guilt in the mind of the detective. But it did not satisfy Dora Darnel. From the first she had made up her mind that her sister-in-law was in some wise implicated in the guilt of that fatal night. She was not going lightly to surrender that belief. It was the fruition of her own evil thoughts, the culmination of her long-cherished dislike of her brother's wife. She was not going to relinquish her own convictions, the outcome of much intense thought, merely because the real criminal had been clever enough to pass some of his plunder to Jaker, no doubt with the express intention of putting justice on a false scent.

While Miss Darnel clung to her own convictions Edward Colchester was pursued by the thought of that handsome and gentlemanlike stranger, whom the Mowbray girls had seen lurking about Darnel. He took occasion to discuss the subject a second time with Miss Mowbray and her sister—during a chance meeting at somebody else's house—and again he heard of the stranger's shabby clothes and superior air, his anxiety to know who was staying at Darnel, and upon which side of the house Lady Darnel's and Miss Darnel's rooms were situated.

"Did he ask about both?" asked Edward, deeply interested.

"Yes, about both. And we were so frightened that we answered him like silly sheep, without thinking how improper it all was," answered Jane.

"Such questions could only be asked by a burglar, could they? And yet he had such a gentlemanly air; and he looked very ill, poor creature," said Miss Mowbray.

"The whole thing is very mysterious," said Mrs. Vincent, the lady of the house, who had called upon Dora Darnel that afternoon, and whose imagination had been fed with suggestions and innuendoes. "But then Lady Darnel is such a very mysterious person."

"She is a charming woman," protested Edward, who was not going to sacrifice Lady Darnel to these ladylike harpies.

He had always liked her and believed in her;

and he was prepared to stand by her now. It was Grace whom he suspected, Grace who had treated him so badly.

"Charming, no doubt. She is very handsome and very elegant, and she has a certain style of her own, which is very taking, even if it is not quite good style," replied Mrs. Vincent, with a judicial air, "but every one must admit that she is mysterious. There is a want of candour, a something underhand."

"Why should you accuse her of being underhanded?" exclaimed Edward. "Did she ever tell you a lie? People are not obliged to go about in society advertising their antecedents. Perhaps she was very poor in her first husband's lifetime, and doesn't care to talk about the shifts she was put to. The world is so snobbish, that people are ashamed of owning they were ever hard up. Or the man may have been a scamp. Who knows?"

"No one knows anything," said Miss Mowbray, maliciously. "Lady Darnel has shown a peculiar talent for holding her tongue."

"Then she is the most original of women," retorted Edward, "and I only wish the rest of her sex were as clever."

This was a glaring piece of injustice, since a few minutes ago he had been doing all in his power to make Jane and her sister talk about their encounter with the tramp, outside Darnel.

But Edward Colchester had not been himself for the last ten days. His heart was gnawed by jealousy, and this gnawing process is apt to have a very bad effect upon a man's temper.

A week had gone by since that morning when Clare Darnel had entered her husband's room, full of love, and hope, to be received with such crushing coldness. She had not seen him since that hour. She had waited meekly till he should summon her to his bedside. She was ready to bear the punishment of her sin against him, that one sin of concealment, ready to acknowledge that she had erred in withholding her confidence from the husband and friend to whom she owed all allegiance.

During the week that was just ended Sir Allan had made marked progress towards recovery. A powerful constitution and habits of exceptional temperance had made his restoration to health easy, when once the bullet had been successfully extracted. He had been gradually regaining strength of body and mind during that week of quiet and seclusion. He had seen his daughter once, his sister three times. Dora had urged her right to see him, and he had yielded to her wish, not without reluctance. She had sat with him for an hour on each occasion, and she had talked softly, in low and gentle accents, yet dropping such drops of venom as those lips of hers were wont to distil when her brother's wife was the subject of conversation. Whatever Sir Allan thought of her insinuations he had been inscrutable.

And now the day had come when he felt himself equal to an interview with his wife—that interview which he felt must needs be final. His house must no longer shelter a traitress, his daughter must no longer call an infamous woman mother. It was to Grace, his only child, his darling of peaceful days gone by, that he turned in this hour of dark despair. Amidst the shipwreck of his happiness she was the straw to which he clung. And now, to-day, when he had to pronounce judgment upon his guilty wife, he summoned Grace to stand at his side, to be, in some measure, judge between him and the woman they both had loved. Grace would incline to mercy. Grace would pity the sinner, even in the midst of her indignation at the sin.

It was the first day upon which Sir Allan had been well enough to sit up for an hour or two. He looked the pale ghost of his old self as he sat by the fire, wrapped in a long brocaded dressing-gown, bordered with sable, as picturesque as the robe of a Venetian senator in the sixteenth century. The gown had been planned and chosen by Lady Darnel, and made in secret, as a birthday gift for her husband. He remembered that fact when his valet handed him the garment, and would have avoided putting it on—but his only other dressing-gown had been stained with blood on the fatal night. He could not reject the obnoxious robe without too plainly indicating his antipathy; and he did not want to make his wife's disgrace common talk in the household.

He sent for his wife and daughter, and they came to him, side by side. Grace flew to the hearth where he sat in a spacious armchair. She flung herself upon her knees beside him and nestled her bright head in his lap.

"Oh, father, what delight to be with you!" she murmured.

Clare stood a little way off, calm, erect, but very pale. If she stood before him thus as a criminal, conscious of that last worst crime of which a wife can be guilty, she was indeed the most audacious among women. But though her face expressed a proud tranquillity, and her eyes, grave, sorrowful, reproachful even, looked at him unshrinkingly, she was content to stand aloof, as one who knew there was an impassable gulf between herself and him. So Allan Darnel thought in his agony, as he looked at the wife he had loved.

Had loved? Is there ever an end to such a love as this? Did Lucius Junius Brutus cease to love his sons when, as their judge, he condemned them to death?

Never had Allan Darnel loved yonder pale beautiful woman more intensely than he loved her now, in this supreme hour of renunciation.

"Grace, I have sent for you because I have that to say to Lady Darnel which I wish you to hear," he began gravely. "There are some fathers who would keep such a sorrow as mine for ever secret from a daughter, who would hush up and gloss over facts, leave all things in darkness and mystery, a something to be wondered about for ever afterwards. But I have chosen to act otherwise. You are a woman, and it can do you no harm to know that there are wicked women in this world as well as good women. I give you my whole confidence, Grace, because I believe you are wise as well as loving."

"Father," cried the girl, looking at him with horror, "what are you going to say? Not one word against my mother."

"Hush!" exclaimed Sir Allan, putting his hand upon her lips. "You must never again call that woman by such a name. You look upon her to-day, I hope, for the last time. Lady Darnel and I are going to part, Grace, for ever. There is no need for me to enter upon the reasons for that parting. She knows what those reasons are as well as I. There need be no public scandal, no disgrace for her—whom we have both loved. Lady Darnel is comfortably provided for under her settlement. She will do well to live abroad, alleging any reason she may please, not dishonourable to me, for our separation. I would spare her all the pain I can, although her infamy well-nigh cost me my life—although her midnight visitor did his best to murder me."

"Father, father," cried Grace, with a wild shriek of horror, "you are wrong—deluded—deceived by me, your wretched daughter. It was in the hope of seeing me that that man came to this house. He had been lurking about all day. He wanted to get an interview with me—to claim my promise—perhaps to ask me for money, since he was brought so low."

"Grace, what are you raving about? You are mad," exclaimed Sir Allan, looking from his daughter to his wife, in sheer bewilderment.

Clare had said not a word. She stood before him silent, imperturbable, waiting to hear his accusation in all its fulness. She wanted to hear him to the end—to learn the lowest depth to which she had sunk in his estimation before she uttered one word in her own defence. And now Grace had come to the rescue—Grace, generous and impulsive—and the whole story must needs be told.

"No, father, dearest, I am not mad; but I have been foolish, blamable, wicked even; for it was wicked to keep the secret of my folly from the best and kindest of fathers. I am deeply ashamed of myself. If that dreadful wound had been fatal I should have been the most miserable creature in this world. I could not have gone on living, knowing that my folly had been the cause of my father's death."

And then briefly, bravely, without disguises or sophistications of any kind, Grace Darnel told the history of her entanglement, told how she had seen her scampish lover upon Chicksand Common when they were out cub-hunting in the morning, and how she had seen no more of him.

"You did not see him again at night, then?" questioned her father. "How do you know that it was he whom I saw in the next room—the man who fired the shot?"

"I do know it—as well as one can know anything from circumstantial evidence—but it is a long story. Hark! there is a carriage," cried Grace, rushing to the window. "It must be the Colonel. I had a letter from him this morning saying he should try to be back to-day. He knows everything. He can convince you that I am telling the truth."

"*He* knows," said Sir Allan. "You trusted him, then, when you dared not trust your father?"

"Because I was not one little bit afraid of him, dear, indulgent, old thing," cried Grace. "May he come upstairs at once? I am dying to see him!"

"Not yet, Grace, we must have this story out first. If—if I have wronged your stepmother as deeply as your words imply——"

"You have wronged her, deeply, cruelly, outrageously. There never was a more devoted wife. I know how she has suffered all through your illness, poor thing; and she stands there like a felon, accused of crimes of which I alone am guilty."

"Clare," cried Sir Allan, holding out his arms to his wife, trying to rise, but almost too weak to lift himself from the capacious depths of the low arm-chair.

"Clare, can you forgive me?"

"Allan, my beloved husband."

She flew to his arms. On her knees, with her head upon his breast, she sobbed out the fulness of her heart.

"No, Allan, no," she gasped, when her passionate tears had exhausted themselves; "no, I am not without guilt. I too have been weak and cowardly. Like this poor girl here, I have had my secret. I have kept one Bluebeard chamber in my life locked from you, the best and most generous of men. Grace is mistaken. Her unprincipled suitor, the unhappy young man who in Paris called himself Victor de Camillac, came to this house on that dreadful night to see me, to obtain money from me—from me whose purse had been emptied for him, time after time, since my marriage. You must have often wondered what I did with my money, Allan, how I contrived to get rid of that handsome income which your love had settled on me. You know now. It was not spent on private charities, as you fancied. It was not from motives of benevolence that I stinted myself of those luxuries women love. It was my worthless son who drained my purse, and squandered your money in gambling clubs and on racecourses."

"Your son?"

"Yes, my son, Stuart Mackenzie's son, who, God help him, has inherited all Stuart Mackenzie's vices, including the capacity for murder. My son, who may before long be standing in the criminal dock to be tried for the crime of that fatal night, and to bring disgrace upon you through your wretched wife. He was not drowned, as we thought, in the *Erl King*. He wrote to me from San Francisco within two months of my marriage. He had seen the announcement in an English paper, and he congratulated me on my good fortune and my power to help him. From that time to this his letters have been one long series of demands. I have complied, weakly, hopelessly, ready to grant anything rather than to let you know my trouble, rather than that you should feel ashamed of your wife's son. He is mine, you know, my very own, my flesh and blood. No dishonour can touch him that does not cast its shadow upon me. I could not bring myself to confess how low he had fallen. If I had told you anything I must have told you all. I preferred to keep my secret, and in this one matter to be a hypocrite."

"Poor Clare! poor misguided Clare! As if I should have failed you, love. Why, I would have stood by you and helped you if you had been the mother of half a dozen scampish sons."

"Ah, you are so good! But I wanted to spare you all trouble and worry."

"And so worried yourself out of health and spirits. All wrong, Clare," said Sir Allan, gently.

"I tried, under these conditions, to do my duty to my wretched boy, tried to be his adviser and guide, to put him in an honourable way of life. I gave him the means of living as a gentleman; the leisure to cultivate the profession of his choice. I refused no request he made me. I lent a willing ear to his promises of amendment. All in vain. He was a drunkard and a gambler—his vices were ingrained in him—a hideous hereditary taint—the leprosy of sin. When he stood before me that night, threadbare, down at heel, haggard, degraded, I knew that he had fallen to the lowest depth of moral and physical ruin. His shaking hands and restless manner told me too plainly that he was a sufferer from his father's old disease, the brandy-drinker's fatal fever. He had so suffered before, as I knew. He had hardly emerged from boyhood when he was first attacked by that horrible complaint. I knew all this, but I did not know that he could be mad enough or wicked enough to attempt murder. He told me of his courtship of Grace—admitted that he had passed himself off as a Frenchman, was daring enough to talk about claiming the fulfilment of her promise directly she came of age. He asked me for a large sum of money, which I refused; and, while I was absent from the room, he opened the Japanese cabinet where you had put the notes—he must have seen you from the balcony—and was in the act of making off with them when you entered."

"I understand," muttered Sir Allan. "It was the money, then, that made him desperate. I had forgotten all about that money."

"Other people did not forget. Miss Darnel brought a detective from London, and he put the whole story together."

"Dora brought a detective here, and without my permission!" exclaimed Sir Allan. "She brought the police into the house while I was lying unconscious here! That was rather a wide stretch of her authority as my sister."

"We were all so anxious about you, dearest,'

murmured Grace. "I daresay it was Aunt Dora's anxiety which made her send for the detective."

"I don't think the whole of Scotland Yard could have done very much towards saving my life, Gracie. It would have been more sisterly of your aunt to have postponed her enquiries till I was able to sanction them."

"She could not have guessed that the thief was my son and Grace's suitor," said Lady Darnel. "Happily for us, the man from Scotland Yard was beguiled by a false scent, and my wretched son is still at liberty. God only knows where he is, and what we may next hear of him."

"Nothing bad, I hope, mother," said Grace, "for the Colonel has undertaken to look after him; and as I had a very cheery letter from the dear old man this morning I have no doubt he has managed everything admirably. Would you mind his coming here now, father? I am dying to know what he has done."

"Yes, Grace, you can send for him now."

Grace went off to deliver her own message, and Allan Darnel and his wife were alone for a little while. Alone, and side by side, full of trust in each other, just as they had been before that crime which for a little while had wrapped their lives in a black cloud.

"Ah, Clare, what a besotted idiot—what a

ruffian I have been to you," said Sir Allan, lifting his wife's hand to his lips. "What shall I do to atone for my brutality?"

"Get well and strong as fast as ever you can, dearest, and let us start upon our journey to the Italian lakes. And—yes—there is one other favour I should like to ask you."

"There is nothing you can ask, love, which I will not grant."

"I think, Allan, when we come back to Darnel it would be better for your sister to find a home elsewhere. I do not believe that she and I can ever be quite happy and at ease under the same roof, for I have an idea that she detests me."

"And upon my honour, Clare, I believe you are right. My sister was a very good sister as long as there was no rival to dispute or share her influence; but she is fond of power, she was proud of her position as mistress of Darnel Park, and she has never honestly forgiven me for marrying again. I believe that, in a lady-like way, she has contrived to prejudice a good many of my old friends against my new wife. She *shall* find another home, Clare. You and I will have nothing but sunshine in our domestic lives. You don't mind Grace, do you? Grace is devoted to you."

"And I am devoted to Grace. I shall be very

sorry when we are obliged to part with her. Oh, Allan, while we are still alone tell me that you can forgive the trouble I have brought upon you through my unhappy son—poor Grace's entanglement—that terrible wound, which has imperilled this dear life. If you had never known me these things might not have happened."

"If I had never known you I should have missed knowing true happiness. We must take the sour with the sweet, the thorns with the roses, dear love. Life is made so. As for Grace, she is a fine, impulsive creature, created to get into mischief of some kind in the flush of youth and folly, like a roe caught in a thicket. And she might have met your scampish son in the Louvre all the same had I never met you."

"Hardly, Allan, for it was your money that gave him the means of living in Paris."

"Here comes the Colonel," said Sir Allan.

Grace came gaily into the sick room, bringing her Indian warrior, whose fine, benevolent countenance beamed with kindly feeling.

"My dear Allan, this is a change for the better. Lady Darnel, I congratulate you," he said, as he sank into the chair which Grace wheeled forward to the hearth. "I was very sorry to leave Darnel while you were in such a critical state; but I had some particular business in town——"

"You can speak before father and mother," said Grace; "they know everything about Monsieur de Camillac."

"I am very glad of that, my dear. First and foremost, then, there are your letters," said the Colonel, handing her a sealed packet. "You can count them by-and-by and see if they are all right. And there is a letter from the young man, whose name is no more Camillac than it is Stukely."

"Grace knows his real name now," said Clare.

"The deuce she does!" cried the Colonel. "It's more than I do, for I believe the fellow has half a dozen aliases. However, Grace knew the man as Camillac, and as Camillac he writes to her, renouncing all claim upon her, acknowledging that he was altogether unworthy of her girlish confidence, and that he obtained her promise under false pretences. The letter was written on board the *Orizaba*, bound for New Zealand, where I have despatched our young friend under the care of a doctor who is going to settle in the colony, and who will look after Mr. Camillac and set him on his legs when he gets out there. If there is any capacity for reform in the man he will have a fair chance of redemption."

"God grant that he may take advantage of it," exclaimed Clare. "Oh, Colonel Stukely, how can I ever be grateful enough to you for this good work?"

"You?" said the Colonel, looking puzzled.

"Ah, you do not understand yet. You have not been told all. The service done for Grace is a tenfold boon to me. The man you have tried to rescue is my son, Valentine Stuart Mackenzie. If you have indeed saved him——"

"If he had been my own son I could not have done anything better for him."

"And you have taken all this trouble, you have spent a great deal of money," began Lady Darnel, but the Colonel interrupted her.

"Don't talk about money. The whole business has cost very little more than a hundred, so far. And that reminds me that I have some money of yours in my pocket-book, Allan, just half of the notes which Lady Darnel's son took in his mad fit. The other half fell into the clutches of Jaker and his brood, who robbed him while he was under the influence of *delirium tremens*. Don't be unhappy, Lady Darnel, the fit was over before we put him on board the *Orizaba*, and my friend the doctor will look after him throughout the voyage. The *Orizaba* is a sailing vessel. The passage will last long enough for a perfect cure, if my friend Feron is as firm as I believe he will be. I put the case in his hands as an interesting experiment. 'Here is a young man organically sound, good looking, well made, well born, well bred, given over to the demon drink. I give him into your custody, out of reach of temptation, for the steward and the captain will work with you for his welfare. You can have him all to yourself for the next two months. If there is any virtue in your science you ought to be able to cure him.' And Feron declared that he would cure him."

Clare gave the Colonel her hand.

"You have brought me comfort and hope," she said fervently. "You are a noble-hearted man, Colonel Stukely, worthy to be my husband's friend."

"You can give me no higher praise than that."

Grace had opened the packet and looked over her letters. Yes, they were all there, the poor little school-girl notes written in the most Britannic French, with much recourse to grammar and dictionary; the letters written later from Darnel, in a freer style, and a little more Gaelic, but abounding in wrong genders and impossible tenses. She glanced through the collection, blushing as she looked, and then knelt down on the hearthrug and threw them behind the burning logs. What a merry blaze they made! While the flames went roaring up the wide old chimney, she turned to her godfather, half in tears and half in mirthfulness.

"You have done something more for me than teach me my catechism and the Ten Commandments in the vulgar tongue," she said. "You have rescued me from a great difficulty."

"Perhaps if I had been in the way to teach you the Ten Commandments, laying a particular stress upon the fifth, you might never have got into that difficulty, my poor Gracie."

"No, if I had honoured my father as I ought to have done I should never have engaged myself to a French art-student without his knowledge," said Grace; and then with a touch of pretty rebelliousness she added, "But then *he* ought never to have sent me to school. That was the beginning of evil."

"That was Aunt Dora's doing," said Sir Allan. "The school was her advice."

"I hate people who are always giving advice," exclaimed Grace. "A thing that costs nothing, and which nobody wants."

How happy they were, sitting round the cosy hearth in the spacious old room which Wren had planned for just such family uses. Four people sitting round the fire in the average modern bedchamber would be a crowd; but here there was room enough for twenty. They sat round the fire talking for the next hour, and almost forgot that Sir Allan was still an invalid, till the family doctor came in and reproved them severely all round, including the patient.

"I said you were to sit up for an hour or so,

and you have been up at least four hours," he expostulated.

"The other three hours went under the head of 'or so,'" replied Sir Allan. "It was a vague expression on your part which I took to have a liberal meaning. Don't be frightened, Danvers, I never felt better in my life; and I am going to eat one of those partridges which you have been pressing upon me as persistently as Louis the Fourteenth upon his confessor. I am going to eat a partridge and drink a tumbler of Heidsieck 'to my supper,' as old-fashioned people say."

"Upon my soul I believe you have been taking Heidsieck already," said the doctor, "for you are as merry as a grig—and you have been all in the dolefuls till to-day."

"The tide has turned, doctor," said Sir Allan. "You shall see how fast a man of forty-five can get well when he is surrounded by those he loves."

Before the end of November, Sir Allan was well enough to start for the south. The day before he left Darnel Park he had a decisive interview with his half-sister, during which he made it very clear to Dora Darnel that her place was no longer under the same roof that sheltered her brother's wife.

"I do not understand in what manner I have offended Lady Darnel," said Dora, with an air of ill-used innocence. "I have absolutely slaved in my desire that everything in this house should be as near perfection as possible. If Lady Darnel had my experience of a large establishment she would be better able to appreciate the trouble I have taken in her behalf."

"Lady Darnel is not unappreciative, Dora. She has a great admiration for your talents as a housekeeper; so great, in fact, that her ambition has been aroused by your example, and she would like when we come back to try her hand at housekeeping on her own account; so I shall be glad if you will plan your future life while we are away. I am sure we shall all be excellent friends at a distance."

Dora paled to the lips, and the hand that played with her watch-chain was faintly tremulous, but she maintained her dignity as she replied:

"I am deeply grateful to you for my release, Allan. Residence under Lady Darnel's roof has long been painful to me. My own wants are of the simplest. My poor little income will enable me to live in London, and in an intellectual atmosphere, where I hope I shall not be misunderstood as I have been here."

"You must allow me to double your income, as I have always intended if ever we came to live apart," said Allan, kindly.

Dora protested against the idea; but there was that in her protestation which assured Sir Allan that she would not be inflexible.

Clare and Grace both left Darnel with lighter hearts because of the knowledge that they would not find Miss Darnel installed there on their return. That pernicious influence would be taken out of their lives for ever.

"I can never forget that it was Aunt Dora who sent me to school," said Grace, in her confidential talk with her stepmother, while Sir Allan slept peacefully on the other side of the railway carriage which was taking them to Genoa. "She is the only person who ever parted me from my father."

"But I believe there is one other person who has the same malicious intention, Grace," answered Lady Darnel, smiling at her. "If Mr. Colchester comes to spend Christmas at Venice with us, as he threatens, I fancy it will be with the hope of persuading you to exchange Darnel Park for the Manor before long."

"He is a most persistent young man," said Grace, blushing. "I hope it won't bore you to have him in Venice."

"I shall be delighted to have him. He has always been my friend. He has never looked coldly upon me as other people have done at Darnel."

"I believe that coldness was mostly Aunt Dora's fault," said Grace, and she was right, for on Lady Darnel's return to her husband's house in the spring, and upon the announcement of Grace's engagement to Edward Colchester, people who had held themselves somewhat aloof before hastened to Darnel to offer their congratulations upon that pleasing event: and somehow before the year was out the neighbourhood began to understand that Lady Darnel was a really charming person, and that Sir Allan was altogether fortunate in his second marriage.

Sir Allan's second wife received all such tardy attentions somewhat coldly, and did not by any means fling herself into the newly-opened arms of the neighbourhood; but Grace's marriage, which took place early in August, brought about festivities and visitings that necessarily drew Lady Darnel into county society. She stinted no splendours or hospitalities that beseemed the marriage of her husband's daughter and heiress with a man of wealth in the neighbourhood; and she bore herself at all these festivities with a quiet dignity which impressed even the doubters.

"Whatever she may have been in the past, she must always have been a lady," said that pleasant old Lady Scattercash, who had enjoyed every hour of her life in London and Paris, before she took to wearing poke bonnets and holding mothers' meetings in Wiltshire; "and that is the main point after all. We don't want to pry into people's past lives, but we cannot receive *ci-devant* barmaids or ballet-girls."

Lady Darnel is so completely happy in her husband's love, and in the perfect confidence now established between them, that she can afford to be very indifferent to the opinions of the county. She has received cheering news from New Zealand, where Stuart Mackenzie has been behaving well and winning friends.

THE END.

PRINTING OFFICE OF THE PUBLISHER.

1400348R0

Printed in Great Britain by
Amazon.co.uk, Ltd.,
Marston Gate.